The World in Elfic Eyes
TRISKELION

Roby R.

This edition first published in paperback by
Michael Terence Publishing in 2022
www.mtp.agency

ISBN 9781800944510

Trinacria Map
by Miriam Garofalo

Cover images
Copyright © bogadeva1983,
Iris Elmo, Peter Hermesfurian
www.123rf.com

Cover design
Copyright © 2022 Michael Terence Publishing

Michael Terence
Publishing

To Gabriele, Miriam and Angelo

SICILY "TRINACRIA"

Sicily is the largest Italian island, one of the pearls of southern Italy, and is bathed by the Ionian Sea, the Tyrrhenian Sea and the Mediterranean Sea.

An island to discover, know and live, between nature, tradition, history and mythology.

And nature seems to have given this land its greatest wonders: mountains, hills, and the sea especially, which with its wonderful colors, the transparency of its waters and the spectacularity of its seabed excels on the other seas.

On this island, the Mediterranean offers scenarios, scents, and flavors that are so unique and intense that only uncontaminated nature can give and do not forget the evocative volcanoes, some of which have never fallen asleep like Etna "A Muntagna" and Stromboli.

A charm also enriched by the precious archaeological evidence that tells the ancient origins of Trinacria (the ancient name of Sicily), and by the many monuments, the testimony of art that has been able to forge over the centuries.

The oldest human traces on the island date back to 12,000 BC, when cultures such as Thapsos flourished. Peoples from the continent settled there later: among them were the Sicans, the Sicels, and the Elymians. In the eighth century BC, we saw Sicily colonized by the Phoenicians and especially by the Greeks, who greatly influenced the history of the island.

The island has a shape reminiscent of that of a triangle whose vertices are:

Cape Pelorus, at the North-Eastern Summit.

Cape Lilybaeum, at the North-West Summit.

Cape Passero "Cape Pachynum", at the South-Eastern Summit.

TRINACRIA
TYI
Cape Lilybaeum
Madoni
Sicans
Mountains
Old Mountains
Krastos
Selinos
Halykos
Akragos
Mo
Hymer
N
W
E
S
MEDITERRAN
SEA

Map by Miriam Garofalo

"Because what I tell you is not just fantasy, but the stories and legends that as a child I lived fascinated, those stories that arise from a land of fire, where sun and sea have been protagonists of myths and legends. This is how my Island is born, adorned with divinities, heroes, nymphs, muses, monsters, wild and luxuriant and lush nature.

And where there is nature there are the elves, the protectors of the mystery of the birth of seed, because nature is magic, and you will discover it with me …"

-Roby R.

Myths and Legends

The legend tells of three magical creatures, three wonderful girls who roamed the world collecting soil and pebbles from the most fertile areas of the earth. One day they stopped at a point where the sea was crystal clear, illuminated by a warm and young sun that reflected all the colors of the rainbow, where the waves sparkled in diamond droplets.

In love with that splendor, they decided to donate the best they had gathered around the world to those wonderful waters, so they began to dance and from their white robes began to spill over the waves, the most fragrant flowers, and the sweetest fruits, especially the most fertile land they had chosen in the most beautiful areas of the planet.

Everything gave the sea, a lot of themselves and from their creativity began to emerge from the boiling waters and the frenzy of the waves a warm, colorful and fragrant land, which would have eternally possessed the secret of the birth of life and nature.

From the points where the three girls had started their dance, the three extreme promontories of the island were born: Pelorus, Pachynum, and Lilybaeum.

Trinacria is born, the magical island where myths and legends remain in the memory of the sky, the sea and the earth and…

Alas, where all this in man falls into oblivion.

Chapter I

From the sea, the Phoenicians sailed towards the fair bay of Naxos. War flags flapped from their cedar boats of Lebanon, red sails furrowed the Mediterranean Sea, presumptuous, violent, pulled by an overpowering wind, perhaps they wanted to announce the blood with which to dye the eastern coasts of Trinacria.

An army of beautiful and valiant beings in glistening green armor waited on the shore with faces turned to the horizon: they were the elves of King Corylus of the Green Valley of Alcantara, the wisest elven king, powerful and brave, ready to fight to honor the pact with men to protect each other.

The elves waited motionless for the signal to hoist their magical bows and shoot their golden arrows at the red armor invaders, and then finish them with the deadly swords; pointy ears ready to catch the slightest signal of their beloved king, while the waves of the sea bathed the calm, tranquil shore, unaware of the blood that would soon be shed.

The battle was near, the village was in danger: the enemy ships were already visible. An elven horn was heard from the shore, announcing the imminent landing of the Phoenician soldiers, who came to destroy that peace made possible by the cohabitation of elves and men. Another horn replied from afar, from the dark forest, warning the Sicel people to run towards the slopes of the volcano, the woods would protect them.

"Runaway, they come!"

Panic broke out: a bustle of frightened people, a frantic race in terror. The Sicels, a population of the Eastern Trinacria, fled to save themselves from the populations they tried in every way to conquer their marvelous and fertile island.

An elf general ran through the crowd with a frown, he ran as he had never done before. People came towards him, running towards the forest, but he was sent to the castle: he had a mission to complete. On Mount Tauro, a hill between rocks and sea, in a unique scenery of variety and contrasts, stood a fortress, where the king of the Sicel Adranos and Queen Thalia reigned, a royal lineage destined to become extinct because without progeny.

Abeius, in his mad dash, thought of all this, he thought that it could not end like this: the men had to fight next to the elves without fear of perishing, protecting the people from the invasion, saving the island from the monster-generating evil. With the volcano in the background, the great Etna that angrily set the sky on fire and echoed with its eruption that seemed to become more and more powerful, the high towers of the castle seemed to catch fire, nothing compared to the eyes of Abeius fixed to scrutinize it, as if to admonish the great volcano. Large walls of black, volcanic stone rose before the elven general. He had never liked that castle, "too black" for his tastes. The big door opened, and he came in so fast that he didn't immediately notice that in front of him, under the arcades, there was a graceful and elegant figure, but with a sad look, Queen Thalia.

"My lady, your people are running towards the woods. An elven garrison will escort them through the forest towards the gorges, the Green Valley of the Alcantara will hide and protect them: my queen Silene awaits for them." Queen Thalia with her deep blue eyes looked at General Abeius, untidy curls fell on her tired but firm face; a light robe covered her with a large, colorful shawl, quickly picked up as soon as she realized the great danger they were running.

"Well. Tuia is ready, King Adranos has climbed the high tower of the north to give her the protection of the stars, then you can take her away."

Queen Thalia spoke cold, almost detached, but Abeius felt that her heart was breaking: since she had been chosen as guardian and protector of the little elf, no woman in the world could be as happy as she was. The woman, whose womb was sterile, had also faced her husband who would never have wanted "the daughter of another", just to be able to take care of the baby.

"Did the king do this? Now I understand the fury of the volcano.

Etna does not approve, fire and Lapilli arrive as far as the Green Valley of Alcantara, and the whole valley could be on fire… However, at the moment, I cannot take care of anything but my mission," he concluded agitated.

Abeius was somewhat bothered by the lack of action of the Sicel king. The men often acted on instinct regardless of the consequences and that gesture could have created some trouble.

Queen Thalia looked down, feeling guilty, but continued to speak firmly:

"The Perseids were waiting to see and bless the little elf, they swarm on her and swarm on the Naxos sky. Their light will fall on the child as a gift of the stars and you should be pleased … After all, the light of the stars is the primordial matter of you, elves."

She looked up at Abeius: "The elven army is already at the bay of Naxos. Abeius, take the child: they must never find her. It could be the end of the elves, of our island, of the world."

A tear fell on her pale face. "King Adranos will escort you to the banks of the Anapo River, to prevent an attack by the Sican people who live in that part of the island. The child must not be seen by any human: she is too rare. The elves have waited so long for her coming, no one has to see her nature, it would be too dangerous."

"Yes, my lady, I will open the portal of time on the river, I cannot guarantee where and at what time I will be able to carry her, but little Greener will live. I will bring her back when the time comes."

"King Adranos is waiting for you at the stables with the little … Let the light of the stars guide you and protect you, General …"

General Abeius, proud in his green uniform, brilliant as an emerald, said goodbye to Queen Thalia who remained motionless and ran away directly to the stables. As the queen had said, King Adranos was waiting for him with a white linen bundle in his arms.

His grim frown, which was frightening just to cross it look and his voice able to make anyone tremble, they had given way to the face of an anxious man, almost moved, who looked lovingly at the baby in his arms.

"She is our hope… Abeius I entrust her to you."

"Yes, Sire."

He snapped to attention, approached and gently took hold of his arms the little one who slept. Then he turned to the king, without fear, with the ruling voice.

"You and your garrison will escort me up at the Anapo river, then you will return to the bay of Naxos and fight alongside my king, His Majesty Corylus: no elf will have to perish for human cruelty. I will keep the great seed of Genesis safe until the day the world needs it … and the little one will live to return when she is ready."

King Adranos delivered a small box in the elf's hands, he turned around with all his royalty and opened the doors of the stables: an army of at least two thousands men on horseback were waiting for him.

Even his majestic black horse burned with the desire to make itself valiant in battle and scratched the ground with its hooves.

The air was suffocating, so thick with tension that it could be cut with a knife. The king's soldiers waited in black armor, whether they wore fear or boldness to face the enemy, nothing leaked from that dark metal in which, at the center of his chest, a large blood-colored dog shone, the "Branchiere", Sicel warrior dog, the symbol of strength and protection.

King Adranos looked proudly at his men and mounted his horse. At his nod, the army galloped after him to follow Abeius. That light elf was like an arrow shot: he passed over land, swamps, woods, and valleys, the wind accompanied him, and he seemed to fly in a race for hope.

Nothing could stop him. In his race for salvation, Abeius could not help thinking of the volcano that threatened, angry, wanted to take possession of the little elf, since she had been stolen with deceit and given to Queen Thalia to raise her as a natural daughter. Everyone would have liked to have her, to exploit her strength, for this no one had to discover her true entity, but of that man, King Adranos, Abeius did not trust.

Among all those thoughts, only one made an overbearing road among the others: Tuia had to live and the portal had to open for her. From afar, after so many, countless kilometers, he began to see the river that shone under the full moon. It was seething when he heard their arrival: a black vortex had opened in the center, hidden by an impenetrable wall of brambles and trees that guarded its secret.

Abeius suddenly stopped and motioned for the king to withdraw. Their eyes met and King Adranos almost feared those green eyes, eyes that once again reminded him to go and fight without fear. The elf said goodbye to the king and his army by bringing his right hand to his mouth and then to his heart, then stepped into the midst of the tall brambles that opened when he passed and disappeared at the sight of the army which, at the signal of their king, he turned around to return to face his destiny besides the elves of King Corylus of the Alcantara Green Valley: fighting the Phoenicians who came to conquer their beloved Trinacria.

Abeius walked briskly through the thick vegetation, brambles and wild thorns did not even dare to touch his armor or his long black hair, indeed the vegetation made way for his passage accompanying him to the bank of the Anapo river.

Finally, he came to the river bank where a frightening vortex roared in the middle of the waters, filtering images of faraway places, of another age surely, but above all screams, breathless sentences and words shaken by pain: a woman was giving birth, the air was soaked from the tension of that moment. Although the vortex was terrifying, Abeius with a quick gesture, stretched out his arms and dropped the baby into those swirling waters. At a time, when the little elf touched the water of the river, the world seemed to end: all of nature screamed in terror from the unexpected gesture.

The wind grew, the lightning lit up the sky and thunder tore through the air. At the center of the river, a typhoon formed and violently swallowed Abeius, disintegrating in a flash of green light. And everything went back quiet on that August evening.

Chapter II

"Abby, we have a problem, you're spreading a little bit too much, the sun isn't filtering, the grass isn't growing, and I … How can I hide?"

A deep voice slid from the tips of a majestic fir tree to the base branches that caressed an 11-year-old girl hidden just below. "Tuia I can't stop growing you know, it's Nature and then you're growing too."

"But I'm a child, it's normal to grow up." Tuia replied, moving to see if anyone could see her from the front window of the building. Gingerly, she began to throw breadcrumbs at the swallows that circled in the sky. If she had caught by her mother would have been a pain, but it was a gesture that she really liked to do.

A series of buildings soared just a few meters from the huge fir tree, planted somehow right there. One thing was certain, it was a great hideout for Tuia, until every afternoon a voice … "Tuia, at home!" It was the mother who called her from the balcony.

So, the girl slipped out of her hiding place under the tree, kept secret by low branches and grass and went up to the fourth floor of the building where she lived with her family.

"Always full of grass … Look, you look like a countrywoman." Mrs Emma had pointed out to Tuia a tuft of grass that hung on her jeans.

"I've been looking for snails, you know there are many little ones around, the ants are back too …"

The mother interrupted her: "Good heavens, I already need the pest control!"

With a violent lash of the head, Tuia turned to her mother blasting her with her bright green eyes: "If it were for you there would be no life on earth! I go to my room."

"And who's waiting for me in the room? That spiteful one of my sister Alice," thought Tuia disheartened.

She slowly opened the door to the room she shared with her two-year-old sister younger than her; indeed, on one of the single beds, sitting cross-legged, there was Alice, a mass of blond curls and clever blue eyes. She played silently with her dolls, after, as far as Tuia had deduced, at first sight, she had turned everything that existed inside the room upside down.

"Alice, but what did you do, I told you a thousand times not to touch my things and specially my books. Ugh!"

The little girl replied angrily: "When you are here you always command, when you are not here I command, is it clear?"

Tuia nodded a discouraged smile: "Never a name was more appropriate: Alice… in Wonderland."

"And you Tuia, what the hell does Tuia mean?"

Alice laughed after her biting joke, not knowing she was leaving Tuia thoughtfully. "Already you have a normal name … Me instead? Tuia is the name of a tree, I read it on the Internet … With so many names, my mother chose Tuia and I don't think she is one who loves nature. And then … why do I talk to a fir tree? Well, maybe I can imagine things! But let it be better studying, I have the last test before the summer holidays."

Actually, it often happened that Tuia thought about it.

Since she was a child, she had been sensitive to any change of season. She smiled at the almond trees in bloom announcing the Spring in Sicily, the mimosa tree for her was a touch of color in that little garden in front of the building where she lived, every year she waited anxiously for the arrival of the swallows that heralded the summer season, she understood when the rain came and she enjoyed dancing under the first September showers.

Autumn for Tuia was magical because the trees were colored and for her, it was a dream, when with her family they went to collect chestnuts at the foot of Etna, very far from the industrialized place where she lived.

In winter she would have liked to see snow, obviously, in Sicily, she sees very little if not at very high altitudes and she lived near the sea, but she found it fascinating to observe the leaden sky over the stormy sea.

Tuia was a small meteorologist: she scanned the sky, she liked to get lost in the immense blue or fantasize among the clouds, she liked to think she could hide behind those grey cushions, she often tasted the air and made her family or classmates angry when she announced that it would soon rain.

She was also very good at school, a model student, but what she excelled in was drawing, she loved nature as much as drawing it and everything she depicted seemed real, alive.

And so, the summer arrived, the swallows had now appropriated the roof of the school, renewing their nests ready for the little swallows. What was Summer for Tuia? Surely she had more time to chat with her friend Abby, the huge fir tree that stood in front of the porch of the building where she lived.

"Abby, why am I talking to you?"

"Because you have nature in your heart."

"But perhaps I only imagine…"

"Um … maybe"

"And why do you talk to me?"

"Because maybe I don't have anyone else to talk to …" And shaking with laughter, the fir tree filled Tuia with twigs.

Tuia often brought up the argument about her doubts, but Abby did not answer, his deep voice hid something.

Tuia's father worked for a company that produced mechanical parts for cars. He was a man in his forties, tall, strong, always smiling and with lots of black hair on his head, very young and lucky to keep such a flowing head due to his age. Lately, he was a bit worried because of the economic crisis that had also affected the stability of the company in which he worked, but always smiling with his daughters and understanding. An inveterate environmentalist, he had transmitted to his eldest daughter the love and respect for nature: they were both vegetarians and with

Tuia, he shared the secret of her hiding place, without however knowing that the daughter was talking to that tree.

One afternoon in late June, back from work, Mr Carlo called his daughter back.

"Tuia come out from there and go home with me, we all have to talk together "He whispered at the base of the tree.

A wrinkle furrowed his forehead and the look of his splendid blue eyes was lost in the void.

The elevator stopped on the fourth floor, Mr Castello opened the armored door and together they entered the apartment.

"Bad news, surely, even my mother is worried." Thought Tuia anxiously.

"Let's sit down, I want to talk to my young ladies."

Alice hopping and humming went to sit on her father's legs, Mrs Emma near Tuia on the sofa.

"Unfortunately, the factory where I work is closing. We workers have chosen to move to another country, to another company or to remain unemployed."

"Unemp … what?" snapped Alice interrupting the man. "Unemployed means jobless, stupid," replied Tuia angry.

"Tuia don't speak to your sister like that," her mother and father reproached her in unison.

"Better stupid than mad! You speak with a tree."

Tuia felt the blood freeze in her veins, her father looked at her and in a low voice: "Tuia you are already 11 years old, enough with the nonsense… This change will help you grow."

Tuia felt her eyes swell with tears; she could no longer speak due to too much anger or perhaps too much sadness.

She could not understand the affairs of adults, everything would change and she would lose her best friend, Abby. She cried all night, remembering the chats with her tree, that distant day when she had slipped under that big fir tree and had heard that warm voice for the first time says to her: "Sweety how are you?"

And then she discovered that it was normal for her to talk to a tree, laugh and joke with him, tell him the anxieties of an interrogation or the fear of a call for some trick done to the little sister Alice. Imaginary or not, Abby was her best friend and lose him hurt her.

The next morning she got up early, put on her short jeans, her favorite pink t-shirt, made a nice ponytail at her long blond hair, took a slice of bread and strawberry jam and left the house barely waving at a nod, the mother who was still in her pajamas.

"She needs time," thought Mrs Emma, pouring a cup of hot coffee.

"Hi Abby, I have to tell you something …" Tuia started, but a lump rose in her throat and she could no longer speak.

"I already know, baby, don't worry. Don't cry. I am here and I will stay here because my roots are firmly planted in the ground, but remember: I am Abeius, I exist, and I will be with you forever."

That deep voice thundered, Tuia's heart trembled with the power of those words. She swallowed the tears together with the words she wanted to say, then something hit her. She looked around and found a small green pinecone, falling from the branches.

"Keep this gift of mine as if it were your life itself and not change. Protect nature and it will protect you … Don't worry I'll be with you."

So, Abby spoke for the last time, leaving Tuia more confused than before. She wanted to know from him who she really was and why he had chosen her.

"Why?"

Now she began to ask herself more insistent questions, many, too many because they filled her mind.

She was different from all the members of her family, more long-limbed, hair growing very fast that in summer became blond as if they ripened with wheat … And then her green eyes: nobody in the world had eyes like hers, so similar to two emeralds, which allowed her to see where other eyes did not arrive.

And she finished school.

Obviously, Tuia had passed her first year of middle school with excellent grades. At home Castello they were all busy for the preparations for the imminent removal and Tuia tried to face everything with strength, trying to "grow" and not to let her father leak out, who was already very worried about the many expenses to be faced.

One day at the end of June, the Castello family finished collecting the last things and left the village where they had lived for ten years.

Tuia could not take her eyes off the big fir tree, which had not spoken since the day he had given her that gift. Maybe she had really grown up and because of this, she couldn't talk to her tree anymore…

In any case, she couldn't do it anymore because her "Abby" was disappearing fast behind a corner of the street.

Chapter III

The new house was not bad: the little sisters each had their room, two very spacious rooms, lit by large windows overlooking the street. From those windows, you could not see lawns, trees or swallows, only concrete and gray houses.

The first night in her new room, Tuia took her pencils and began to draw trees. She could only draw those, large, leafy, bare, flowery, fir, almond, mimosa that she could also smell, and every completed drawing was hung on the walls of her room until she felt exhausted into a deep sleep.

A green light filtered through a small box; a whisper woke her up: "Tuia."

The girl got up from her desk and went to see why that light was calling her. She opened the box and the light wrapped it in a whirlwind of lightning. The small pinecone was floating in front of her.

"Little Tuia, your day will come soon. Someone is waiting for you and you will discover your past, your present and your future. I am with you."

It was the voice of her Abby, Abeius had spoken to her, somehow and who knows why, from what seemed to her an insignificant little pinecone. A tear fell on her cheek: hearing that beloved voice warmed her, driving away from the sadness. Suddenly, the room door snapped open and Alice entered crying and screaming that she had a bad dream with monsters and bad people.

"I want to sleep with you," her little sister sobbed and fell asleep on Tuia's bed.

Tuia didn't understand if her confusion depended on the fact that she had suddenly woken up or for the mysterious dream she had made. The small pinecone remained inert inside the little box on the bedside table.

The summer was already in full swing, a heavy heat was

suffocating the entire country that remained deserted because its inhabitants preferred to cool off at the sea. Even the Castello family was a frequent visitor to the beach, they were all more serene, especially Mr Carlo who had overcome his crisis, the only one with her head still in the clouds was Tuia.

“Tomorrow we go to Pantalica,” began Mr Castello.

“It’s Mid-August and especially, it’s Tuia’s birthday, we will celebrate there.” Tuia jumped into her father’s arms, hugged and kissed him hard. She loved that place, Tuia really worshiped it: so much nature, wild nature, the noise of the Anapo river…

It would have been an unforgettable day. And then it was her birthday, better than that it couldn’t go. She looked with love at her father and mother and knew that this was their birthday present, nothing could be more welcome.

Chapter IV

The car was ready, full of lunch and everything that could be used to spend a wonderful day in Pantalica. Tuia was excited and couldn't stay seated in the back seat. Not even the singing/shouting of Alice bothered her, her eyes would finally see the green again.

She already saw it, that place that she felt like home … Often she had fantasized about the many caves that opened onto the great canyon carved by the Anapo river, over the shady and wildly scented forest where the brambles protected access to the dark and mysterious caves. Certainly, a Necropolis where there are as many as five thousand tombs dug out of the rock, it should have frightened a girl of eleven, but Tuia would have gladly visited those niches, curious to build fear stories to tell her sister and friends. One thing was certain: that day would have been wonderful, on her birthday between the river, the woods and the blue sky.

Finally, the Castello family had arrived at an open space where they could park the car and then continue on foot through steep paths that descended steeply into the valley. Tuia breathed and tasted that air, filled her eyes looking at the nature around her, listened to the river flowing at the bottom of the valley.

The descent through the paths, where one had to be careful not to get caught in the brambles, was a pure adventure for Tuia while Alice had already fallen a couple of times stumbling over some small pebbles, peeling one knee and crying loudly.

"Be quiet, you have nothing. You will see that the water of the river will heal you," Tuia annoyed tried to encourage her sister, more than anything else to silence her and be able to hear the flow of the river, the birds and all the sounds of that magnificent place, until…

"Tuia."

A light whisper, almost imperceptible, went to caress the little girl's neck, she shivered. Recovering from that moment of loss, she turned abruptly to look towards the caves but saw nothing.

The moment she was about to resume following the path she seemed to see something inside one of those cubicles carved into the rock. She shivered again, tried to look better, but saw nothing … Was it a reflection of the river's waters or had someone called her?

The day passed calmly; the river was wonderful, you could see the stones at the bottom and some little fish swimming peacefully, except when Alice with her net was trying to catch it, but Tuia made it run away first, sending her little sister into a rage. There were natural arches of dense vegetation that made some corners of the valley shady, damp as if the sun was forbidden to enter and peek. Plane trees, willows, poplars and other species of trees made everything almost fairytale and Tuia often remained enchanted watching them, feeling lucky to live on the most beautiful island in the world.

It was late afternoon and the little family was already starting to prepare for the return home. Tuia began to feel sad, her little sister had fallen asleep on a mat and her mother had covered her with a beach towel, the air, in fact, began to get a little cooler. Now the sun illuminated only a part of the valley, focusing on some caves and the niches that faced it.

The girl decided to take a last bath in the river, before drying herself and leaving to return to the gray village. While Alice slept, Tuia would have finally taken the opportunity to hike near the caves and tombs and maybe go and peek inside one of those niches where she had imagined hearing her name called.

She started to climb the path and infiltrated the narrow vegetation. To her great amazement, she passed quietly without being scratched by thorns, her colorful costume did not get caught between thorns. It almost seemed as if the brambles moved as she passed. She arrived almost immediately in front of the small niche that intrigued her and there she heard it again: "Tuia…"

At that point she had no more doubts: the whisper was real, it could not be her imagination. She gathered all her courage and answered, "Here I am" and entered.

Dark, wet, an embrace of warm air enveloped her, surrounded her, caressed her like a caress. Tuia remained motionless, unable to speak or do anything, only felt that something inexplicable was happening to her.

She was still, but she seemed to be moving quickly: the dot of green light she saw in the distance approached, getting bigger and bigger until blinded her.

As soon as Tuia opened her eyes she realized that she was no longer in her Pantalica and that a rather strange man was in front of her. He was kneeling in front of her and he looked like a soldier with a green, precious armor that reminded her of ancient ones.

He raised his head and beautiful emerald green eyes pierced her. Tuia, scared, tried to run back, where she thought she had come from. In a leap, the mighty arm of that man grabbed her as he tried to reassure her with a calm voice: "Stop."

"I know this voice …" Tuia muttered to herself. She turned to tears and shouted: "Abeius … Abby, are you?"

The soldier stood up, with a loving smile on his face, eyes bright with happiness, opened his arms, waiting.

All that was happening to her was madness, but she didn't think twice: she had smelled the fir tree with which she had grown and all the confidence he gave her, she was sure it was her Abby and ran to him.

Abeius held her tightly against him, happy to have finally returned in his elven form, but worried because now everything became more complicated and dangerous.

Tuia left Abeius and stood looking at him, contemplating him and noticed that he was not a man, not a normal man anyway.

"Abeius what are you? Oh, sorry, what kind of human do you belong to?" Perhaps she was impertinent, but now Tuia wanted answers. "I don't belong to any human race. I am an elf, I am

General Abeius, of the army of the falcons of King Corylus and Queen Silene of the Green Valley of Alcantara and I will be the protector of your journey. "Abeius answered proudly in the high uniform of a general.

Tuia watched him as he spoke. He was beautiful, tall, had bronze skin, long black hair, wonderful green eyes and strange pointed ears that made her smile.

He had a splendid uniform, with a golden peregrine falcon head engraved on his chest, a huge sword she could not even lift. He looked like a Greek soldier, like those she had studied in history books, but she had never seen one so beautiful.

"You are Tuia Orientalis, carry the great seed of Genesis with you, you will know along the way the guardians, the green-eyed Greeners, the noble lineage from which you come and along your journey you will understand yourself. Your story begins in an age without age that human memory did not remember, does not remember and will never remember; only the earth, the sky and the sea hide the truth of the origin of this island, a great emerald in the Mediterranean Sea. The noble elves adorned it with proud trees and the best fruits, under the watchful eye of the great volcano, her majesty, the Etna. Because nature is the real magic, remember Tuia."

At those words of her elf friend, Tuia looked at him confused, but instantly her mind opened, and something began to seem clearer to her: the puzzle of her life slowly began to take shape, but there was still something that didn't it was clear.

"Abeius, but I have human parents, isn't it? How can I be an elf?"

"I had to protect you from the great war, between men and elves … I made sure you were born into a human baby and that your human mother called you with an elven name. Your entity grew up with the child Tuia."

"And why were you a tree?"

"I am a Greener, a guardian, the Greeners represent the elements: air, water, fire and earth. I am the guardian of the latter and I keep the primordial secret of life. A Greener has no parents, it is the matter itself that generates it. I was a tree because my mission was to be near you, to cultivate in you the love of nature, to protect yourself. I will be your guardian and I will teach you to know your entity until you develop the strength to dominate the element."

While Abeius spoke, Tuia looked around. The place was strange, lit by a white-green light; the air was still as if they were inside something.

"Abby, what is this place? Tuia finally said, trying to understand, looking also behind her at the undefined place where she was.

"We are in a temporal limbo. Coming out of here I'll take you in to your era, your human past remote, but it's your true elven present." Abeius looked at Tuia in the eyes and saw fear and insecurity.

"Do not be afraid, I will be with you, as I always have been, even when you did not see me, I was there."

"It's not true, I cried a lot, I cried alone … and you, where were you? Now I understand why I felt so different."

"I lived in that little pinecone that you kept with love and that you brought with you today, tied to a necklace."

Tuia looked at the necklace she had created with string, to which she had tied her precious pinecone, made to always have it with her and to prevent her sister from taking it and losing it.

"One last thing … From the moment we exit the time portal, your appearance will change. Don't fear changes, changes are always positive."

And so Abeius took Tuia by the hand and together they crossed that wall of light.

Chapter V

A warm sun greeted Tuia and Abeius, who had come from who knows where, but General Elf knew that place very well.

Tuia still kept her eyes closed, partly from fear but also because the light was really blinding.

"Where are we now?" said the girl, a little curious and a little anxious.

"Don't open your eyes. Breathe deeply and listen, you will hear familiar noises and new ones, but your feelings will reveal the place to you."

Tuia felt a noise, a coming and going of feet that trod the ground and pebbles, but also the rustling of the air among the leaves of the trees, the chirping of birds, the flow of a stream, perhaps a river … So many familiar smells, of damp, of wild herbs, butcher's broom, hawthorn and wild garlic flowers; it was impossible for her not to recognize them because they brought her back to …

"Pantalica! Are we in Pantalica?"

She opened her eyes and gasped.

"Well Tuia, we have already tested your senses … Yes, we are right in Pantalica and it is the city that you are at this moment admiring in your true present, with its life and its history, but with its king particularly. This is the kingdom of King Anax who lives in the great castle on Mount Lauro, the majestic Anaktoron."

Abeius opened his arms and showed the kingdom of Pantalica to a confused and surprised Tuia in noting that, where she knew there was only grass, trees and brambles, there was a city in her time.

What an emotion! The valley swarmed with elves who went back and forth in their daily affairs; the city was made up of houses dug out of the rock and huts that came out from under huge trees, hidden by willows, poplars or brambles themselves, in perfect harmony with the wild nature around, bathed by the rivulets of the Anapo that flowed undisturbed in the middle to so much "elf" civilization.

At the bottom of the valley, near the river, there was a market and from the hill Tuia could smell the vegetables and fresh fruit, half-open red watermelons could be stockpiled from above, as well as strawberries, cherries, plums, peaches and even tomatoes and the smell of basil and oil rose strongly to the nostrils and made one think of a Summer of genuine flavors, the flavors of her island.

Her eyes were not enough to enjoy that splendid view, she savored that air which tasted of good things and not of modern polluting industries.

"This is my island," thought Tuia with all her soul, filling her eyes and lungs with everything that this spectacle of nature was giving her.

"See, this is the world you belong to. Unfortunately, you will discover that something has gone wrong … But before that, you have to learn to be an elf."

Abeius looked at Tuia with a little smile, which she didn't understand. The general was already seeing the first signs of change in the girl's body, signs that indicated that the young elf had returned home.

"Now we'll take a ride. Obviously, we are foreigners and we will not go unnoticed, but we avoid chatting with people and not saying who you are … Later we will have to see someone who will prepare you to meet the king."

All around it was full of elves, all busy in their daily life. Young elves, women and men, very few elders and not children at all.

"Where are the children, Abeius? Everyone here is happy and serene, but I only see adult elves, men and women … Little elves must be beautiful, I think … Isn't that so?"

"Yes, they are…"

The general said no more. He seemed a little uncomfortable because of those questions, something troubled him, but Abeius knew that the time would come soon to reveal everything to Tuia, that little elf so important.

The walk through the stalls was very funny for Tuia: she enjoyed the colors of the seasonal fruits they gave her and she did not hesitate to eat them because tastes so genuine she had never tasted, she also savored some sweet figs, which reminded her of the ones she brought her the beloved grandfather who was no longer there.

The biggest surprise was when, in a small square, she saw hearths where they were cooking tomatoes: some elves mixed huge cauldrons where a heady sauce boiled while others prepared jars for preserves, all cheered by tarantellas played and danced from musician elves.

"Abeius, how beautiful preserves are! It is a tradition on our island to prepare tomato sauce and bottle it in the summer, but won't it be an elven tradition?"

She ran to look inside the cauldrons where the tomatoes boiled, releasing a very good perfume. Then she approached the players, to contemplate the ancient finely carved musical instruments; the music was intense and eloquent, it told of myths and legends, the drums beat inside Tuia's chest, dragging her away into those ancient and cheerful notes.

And so, it was that Tuia captured by music and perfumes began to dance, a cheerful dance that brought her back to ancient days, to the memories of a land that lived inside her. The flames of the hearths seemed to dance with her, filling the air around red lapilli that floated beside her. Abeius looked at her stunned by such beauty, almost hypnotized by her movements, as were all those present who circled around her as if that dance were to last forever. The smoke rose from the hearths and the flames grew to the rhythm of music until they grew high to create an arc around Tuia, dangerous.

Suddenly Abeius awoke from that enchantment, ran to Tuia, took her by the arm and took her away. The general knew that the dance was about to reveal dangerously the identity of the girl. At least now he was sure of the element that Tuia dominated.

They left that corner of flavors and fragrances, which returned to normal and continued along the cobbled street that passed the fair, they walked a little along a stream until they reached a grove, quite dark and damp, tangled with bushes, where however the Anapo river had no trouble flowing quietly.

They went into that wild darkness; they had no difficulty seeing because an elf's eyes can see through the darkness and notice anything without problems.

At one point they found themselves in front of a small clearing, like a farmyard, dominated by a huge weeping willow that looked like a large palace. At its feet, hidden by the shadow of the lush foliage, was a woman sitting.

Certainly, a somewhat strange woman, dressed all in black lace, who leaned her back on the side of what looked like a door that came out from under the big tree. Sitting with one leg dangling, with the other she stretched out to touch the opposite side of the door with her foot, while quietly smoking an ancient pipe engraved with mysterious idioms, from which the smoke rose upwards with strange twirls.

She didn't move, she looked at Tuia and Abeius coming to her under a blanket of curly black hair and when the two visitors arrived in front of her, she looked up and two powerful black eyes pierced them.

She examined them with a deep look, almost inspecting every corner of their body until she stopped to stare closely at Tuia's eyes. The girl tried to avoid those piercing eyes; the woman really gave her so much awe, but when she looked away, trying to escape from those disturbing black eyes, the woman spoke: "Well, I've been waiting for you, General. Had you a good trip? Meanwhile revenue, we have a lot to talk about and it is better to avoid the prying ears of some small nosy person."

At those words, there was a small moan and a rustling from behind a bush as of an animal that discovered flees away. Tuia and Abeius turned to look but saw nothing but a movement of leaves.

Meanwhile, the woman had entered her home, which seemed more like a den to Tuia. From that willow, you could access a grotto elegantly carved in limestone, illuminated by the lights of candles that popped out from all sides and reflected on a vaulted roof. Large red pillows filled one side of the room, everything was elegant and fragrant with flowers and aromas, basil, mint and thyme grew naturally on the sides of the cave and wild cyclamens colored the edges of a small stream that flowed inside.

The woman went to lie down on the big cushions and motioned for the guests to do the same. Tuia couldn't wait to rest and literally dived in the middle of that comfortable couch while Abeius stood to wait, almost anxious to start the conversation.

"I'm Gabrys, I'm a druid, a witch."

She turned to look at Tuia intensely.

"I was born a few centuries ago in distant northern islands like all the elves living on this island and your arrival is a sign to me that indicates that the return to my land is approaching. Now my duty is to prepare you to meet his majesty King Anax, my great friend, but I warn you: most likely it will not be a happy visit." The witch was very determined in her manner of speaking, which indicated a strong and sure character.

Abeius had heard of her once, in a story that told of the elven curse and a powerful witch called "the bat."

Meanwhile, Tuia had fallen into a deep sleep due to her fatigue.

"Do you know that the girl I have with me is not a normal elf?" Abeius was anxious to bring the subject up to what he was interested in.

"Of course, I know who she is: the last-born elf. The curse could have stopped the procreation of the elves, but not the stars … I know her entity and I know that you know it too. Obviously, she is a guardian, a Greeners like her wonderful green eyes show, but she will have to discover herself; no one can reveal what her element is, she will have to find out for herself."

The witch Gabrys answered Abeius with certainty, she knew more than the elf general could imagine.

"Only the last-born elf can free the elven people from the curse. I saved her from the treachery and greed of a king, I will continue to protect her with my own life. I've been ready for my mission for a long time."

The general at attention touched his lips and heart as an oath to his words, but inside him, he knew very well that Tuia was already carrying her in his heart and he didn't need to swear anything.

Chapter VI

It was barely dawning, though no light shone from the hanging branches of the willow. Tuia was awakened by the smell of fresh fruit, warm milk and fried donuts.

"Um, how hungry! Good morning, sorry but last night I was too tired … I also had a strange dream where there were the sea, strange monsters, and a dragon."

Hungry she grabbed a hot donut and stuffed it in her mouth, busy as she was to gorge herself as if she had never eaten in her life, didn't notice that Gabrys and Abeius had looked nervously at her last words.

"Hurry up, we have to move before the sun has risen completely." Gabrys urged Tuia and Abeius to hurry up, collecting breakfast and putting it in a raw linen bag.

"This will serve us."

Quickly she slipped into a hole in the opposite wall, which turned out to be a tunnel at least seventy meters long that climbed up and up steeply.

Finally, having faced that intense climb, Gabrys stopped; they had arrived in a large cave that opened at least three hundred meters above the valley, there was a slight brightness outside: the sun was rising.

"This is the Faria cave." Gabrys showed the place where she had brought her guests, bustling about to store her luggage on either side of the dark cave. At the center of the cave, there was a circular excavation full of water and Gabrys had Tuia positioned on the edge of the small pool, in front of the cave opening.

"Lux," the witch murmured, throwing a bright red powder into those calm waters.

A blade of light crept in from the opening of the cave and ran towards Tuia, who looked at it curiously until it touched the water. The light expanded throughout the cave.

Tuia looked into that pond and saw herself reflected; it wasn't her, but there was a girl with long red hair, tall and with pointed ears, the girl had given way to a beautiful young female elf.

Marvelous, with wide-open eyes and wide-open mouth Tuia, could not react to that sight, then Gabrys spoke to her:

"Dear Tuia, this is your true appearance. Forget about the child you were, now the Trinacria needs you. A curse makes the elven people sterile, you are the last-born elf, only you can save the elves and consequently your beloved island. Elves are nature, life … without them, everything ends. Before you have your first menstruation, you will have to recompose the Triskelion, symbol of the Trinacria, destroyed by the dragon Typhoeus. Maybe so everything will be back in its place."

At that moment the witch feels unconscious but almost uttered her last words in a whisper: "And my home."

The light had now invaded the whole cave, Tuia was still stuck in herself; she never stopped staring at herself in the water, she was a beautiful girl, or rather a beautiful female elf, and she wore a white linen dress with ankle-strap leather sandals.

She tried to stop gazing at herself and go to help Gabrys, who was gradually recovering, but by then she was so fascinated by her new appearance and how quickly she had grown that she didn't even notice that Abeius was looking at her in amazement.

Tuia raised her eyes and crossed those of the general, blushed embarrassed, the only thing she could say was: "I grew up, eh!"

"Yes," Abeius replied dryly, not knowing what to add.

"My bag … where is my bag?"

A groan rose from poor Gabrys, who was regaining consciousness.

"I have to eat; I have to recover my strength … Then we'll talk."

So, in the warmth of morning sun, the three finally had a good and abundant breakfast.

Chapter VII

Tuia ate in silence. She felt observed, she knew that now the time would come when she would have to act "when she was grown-up" she who had always hated the things of the grown-ups, now she had to behave as an adult.

"What is the Triskelion?" She asked point-blank.

"The Triskelion is the symbol of your land, the symbol of the Trinacria. It has the shape of your island, formed by the three headlands Pelorus, Lilybaeum and Pachynum, born from the magic dance of three elves. For your journey, you will have to get the information from that story … So, you'll find out how to act. "Gabrys replied.

She ate her breakfast but, in the meantime, she stared at Tuia, checking every one of her reactions: she wouldn't let the little elf have any panic attacks listening to what they were revealing to her.

"Abeius, but I don't know where to go … I know every story and every ancient legend that concerns my land but are they not just myths?"

She paused a moment to think and then continued: "Thinking of it, for how things are, maybe not … OK, I'm ready, tell me how and where I have to go."

Tuia stood up firmly, encouraged by the fact that she knew her Island well. She would be guided by those legends and would have followed the ancient maps that had always attracted her.

Gabrys looked at her in wonder, she didn't imagine so much strength of spirit and courage from a "child."

Tuia stood up, heading for the pond dug out of the cave. As soon as she passed by, a monstrous hand made of mud grabbed her head, trying to drag her into a black vortex. Only the speed with which Abeius drew his sword and cut off that evil limb prevented Tuia from being swallowed by the vortex.

Tuia was shocked, Gabrys immediately threw herself into the little lake where the vortex had closed bringing with her the sliced limb and began to scrutinize the water remained murky.

"Abeius, unfortunately, they took the child," she said in shock.

"What? What child?" Tuia, recovering from the shock, turned to the witch, searching for answers.

"The child Tuia was caught by an ambush by Ceto, the sea monster. She failed to kill her because the real Tuia is here with us, but the child fell into a deep sleep … I believe she took her mind."

Gabrys continued to look carefully into the pond and an image began to emerge so clear that Abeius and Tuia could understand what was happening.

"I see the child being rescued by her human parents … She will not die, but she will not awaken until her thoughts are released."

Tuia remained for a while in thoughtful silence. Something clear was about to reveal itself in her mind; all the ancient legends and myths of her island returned to memory but the image of the Trinacria specially.

"For the stars in the sky, the one who tried to take me away was Ceto, the sea monster mother of the Gorgons? I begin to tie the story … And I already know the symbol of the Trinacria. Come on, Abeius, we must find Ceto, the limb that you have cut her and free my mind from those horrible monsters."

A particular trait of Tuia's character was precisely the courage to face situations with decision, and together with stubbornness and, certainly, a part of unconsciousness that the youth gives, was just what could save people sometimes.

Abeius looked at her proudly. She was determined as a true elf, but first, she had to learn to defend herself, to shoot with the bow as only the elves can do and to handle the sword. Her path was proving more dangerous than he could have imagined, the oldest sea monsters awaiting her, Ceto and Phorcys and a curse to be destroyed.

Chapter VIII

"Tuia! Tuia, wake up, I'm your mother … Carlo doesn't answer she hit her head!"

After hours of research, Tuia had been found by her parents on the riverbank, unconscious and with a bleeding head.

The Castello family had immediately given the alarm, not seeing Tuia arrive after calling her to go home; the research had started almost immediately, mainly because the light at the end of the canyon was thin, the evening progressed and soon it would be dark.

Alice cried without comfort, even more, when she saw her sister immobilized and taken to the nearest hospital.

The doctors tried to reassure their parents: in reality, Tuia had fainted, had a slight wound to the head, but did not wake up … What was the reason, they still did not know.

"Dad, is Tuia dead?"

Alice frightened and her eyes swollen with tears, she asked her father and mother what was happening to her older sister.

"No, she sleeps," replied the confused but very worried mr Castello, turning a frightened look on his wife. "All we can do wait for her to wake up."

Mrs Emma took the hands of her daughter Alice and her husband and together they went to sit in the waiting room of the intensive care unit where Tuia had been hospitalized.

A dark shadow hung over the little Tuia in the world of men, held her trapped in dreamless sleep, a sleep that modern human science was unable to understand. What they could have understood would have been the dark wickedness that had generated it, the same wickedness and brutality that had led the world to wars and the destruction of most of the human race.

Meanwhile, in another reality, the elves betrayed by humans

decided to abandon men to themselves, to their self-centeredness and their innate self-destruction.

Chapter IX

Isolated by men, the elves lived in remote areas of the Trinacria, impassable valleys, hidden by woods and mountains, in a valley of these rose the city of Pantalica where a king reigned. His palace was called Anaktoron, a fortress on Mount Lauro, sheltered from the cold north winds and overlooked the great canyon carved by the Anapo river.

The king who lived in this great palace, inaccessible from looting and incursions of foreign peoples, was called Anax and long meditated revenge against an elven general who had been the cause of the loss of his family.

The first of August night many years before, the annual festival of the sea and stars was celebrated, all the elves had gathered in Thapsos to pray to the Perseids, the island's protective stars, to free them from the curse that made them sterile.

The Thapsos peninsula was the place where the stars and the sea met and all the elves of the island went dancing the dance of genesis, the ancient one that gave rise to the life of the island.

That night a meteor darted in the dark sky and fell on the great volcano Etna with a great roar. A long red glow emanated from the volcano, then everything returned to normal and the elven people continued with its celebrations, unconscious that, meanwhile, the dragon Typhoeus that lived inside the volcano, had received a gift from the Dragon's constellation. For centuries he had waited for the moment that would mark the end of the extinction of his species and now, finally, near the great crater the meteor had left him a … new-born.

"A new-born?"

Typhoeus was disappointed, but he understood that this was the choice of the stars and he could not oppose it. His imposing size, with his hard-golden scales, could not possibly demand delicacy, but he took the helpless little creature in the palm of a paw from the deadly claws and carried it into his ardent cavern.

She was an elf-born baby and Typhoeus knew that she would become a powerful guardian because she had wonderful eyes of an emerald green that only the Greeners had. She was his and he would have stained with blood anyone who took her away from him.

Meanwhile, an elven general had been sent by his king to see what was happening to the volcano. When he reached the slopes of Etna, he noticed that a woman was running exactly towards the crater.

"Queen Thalia! Where are you going? It's dangerous here for you, the dragon could capture you!"

General Abeius immediately stopped the woman who seemed desperate.

"He took it! He took my baby!" said Queen Thalia distorted.

"Did the dragon take your baby?" Excuse me majesty, but you … you can't have children."

Abeius began against his will almost to doubt the queen's lucidity.

"I prayed desperately for the stars to send me a daughter and they satisfied me tonight, but the dragon caught her! She will die if I do not take her away with me!"

So, the woman threw herself at the elf's feet calling for his help. Abeius, embarrassed, took Queen Thalia in his arms, comforted her and placed the shawl over her shoulders.

"Queen Thalia, stay hidden here, I'll go see what it is. He looks calm in there; the dragon will be sleeping."

So silently and quickly as a cat in the night, Abeius went into the fiery pit of the beast and realized with astonishment that next to the enormous dragon a baby really slept. He approached without making any noise and picked up the small bundle that opened her eyes instantly.

At that moment the general was invaded by terror: if the child had started screaming, the dragon would have devoured him in a second. But she remained quiet and looked at him with her gleaming emerald green eyes, unmistakable eyes that indicated that the baby was a future guardian. He ran out of the cave and walked away, reaching the place where he had left Queen Thalia.

"Here is the little girl, your majesty," said Abeius anxiously, handing the little elf into the arms of an impatient Queen Thalia.

"But it is a small elf! And what's more … Abeius you looked at her, she's a Greeners."

Queen Thalia looked lovingly at the baby she held tightly in her arms as tears of joy streaked her face.

"This complicates things … No one among humans will have to know the identity of the child, they could kidnap her to exploit her power." Abeius's words were full of anxiety.

"Who would ever dare touch the king's daughter?" Queen Thalia replied firmly and took the road that led down to her palace in Naxos.

Abeius was not convinced but he decided to escort the queen to her palace: she and the little elf had to arrive healthy and safe. Then that baby was too important, she was the last-born elf and she would surely have marked the fate of the elven people.

Almost arrived at the palace of Naxos, Abeius and Queen Thalia were hit by a chilling roar and fiery lapilli from the crater of Etna: the dragon Typhoeus woke up.

Furious at not finding the child, his little jewel, he began to spit fire and roar madly, waking the flames of the great volcano that began to roar irate, causing dangerous earthquakes. His green snake eyes scanned the flames that revealed the appearance of the intruder, of the thief who had dared to take away his little elf from him.

"A despicable elf has dared to steal my precious gift! The elven people will then cry! Their sufferings will be three times greater than mine."

Thus, angry and mad with grief, he left the crater and flew off, driven by the flames of the lava that now burned and descended over the Etna valley, burning down everything he encountered on the street. Typhoeus began to fly southwards, towards the

Thapsos peninsula, where he knew he would find the elven people in celebration.

A terrible roar and a great roar struck hit the elves intent on celebrating the stars, who suddenly saw themself attacked by a huge giant of golden scales with eyes burning with anger.

All the elves who were in front of the dragon ran terrified towards the coast trying to dive into the sea to save themself, but Typhoeus was very fast and took three with his claws. The cries of prayer and despair of the other elves were of no use for him to release them: he was so furious that in a moment he took off and quickly returned to the volcano.

Arriving on Etna, the dragon Typhoeus sealed the crater with an incantation, he left the elves to live prisoners in his cave and he fell into despair, losing the desire to live day by day.

When the dragon was away and the elves tried to somehow comfort themselves, one man could find no comfort, and that man was King Anax to whom the dragon had taken away his wife and two daughters.

After that tragedy King Anax quickly grew old due to the great pain and anger that invaded his soul, becoming perhaps the only old man that could be seen among the elves. He wore himself out further when he found out from his faithful seer who the elf was that had provoked the dragon's fury, meditating every day of his life to take revenge.

That day had arrived, he had learned that the elf he was expecting had arrived in his kingdom along with a young elf. It could only be him, because there were no young elves all over the island and he was waiting for him determined to wash with his blood years and years of painful suffering.

Chapter X

Gabrys gave herself no peace. She talked to herself and went back and forth to the Faria cave, stopping every so often only to start walking again with her forehead more frowning than before.

"They know that the last-born elf is here to free the elven people from the curse. They fear it, Ceto and Phorcys will not stop and now they have something really precious in their hands. But what do they have to do with the Triskelion?"

"I'll tell you," Tuia began, rising from the ground, where she sat in silence, thinking of everything that was happening to her.

"Legend has it that Ceto and Phorcys were two brothers, two monsters of the primordial human history, sons of the sea and of the earth. Ceto married Phorcys and had children including Scylla, Echidna, the *Graeae*, the Gorgons and Ladon, monsters who lived on the seabed. Apparently, it's not a legend, it's my reality. The symbol of the Trinacria is born precisely from three of these monsters and for what I understood who will have to do them outside is really me."

Abeius and Gabrys looked at Tuia open-mouthed: they would never have imagined everything the girl was revealing to them.

"You, Abeius, have already carried out the mission by cutting a limb in Phorcys, which we must recover, so there are two more to rebuild the Triskelion."

The witch and the general had gone pale. They knew it was true, she came from the future earth, but they certainly knew that what the girl said was extremely dangerous to implement.

"In the meantime, let's go, it's getting warm here and I can't stand all this light. We'll go down to my house and get ready to meet the king and it won't be a kind welcome. It's not the time to talk about it now." Gabrys picked up her bag a little worried and started the tunnel descent, muttering to herself. Tuia and Abeius followed her, the general still holding his sword, now ready for anything seen the last events.

The descent was steep, with a sharp elbow bend that led to the other side of the valley that was going to come out in front of the "house" of the witch Gabrys, called "Cave of the bats", perhaps because the mistress was always dressed in black or perhaps because a colony of these nocturnal mammals dwelt right under the great willow tree, which hid its entrance.

As soon as the witch put her foot out of the tunnel, she was stopped by about twenty elves on horseback; their spears also blocked Tuia and Abeius who immediately had to put down his sword.

One of them approached and dismounted by his horse. He had a shining silver armor, with a hawthorn's crest on his chest. "I am Salix, general of King Anax of the kingdom of Pantalica. I am here by order of the king: I must lead you to the palace, his majesty wishes to meet you urgently."

Gabrys looked around suspiciously, already imagining how the king had known Tuia's arrival so quickly and it was not long before she discovered the alleged spy among the branches of a poplar tree. "Rosewood, come down, bad spy."

A small man covered, or formed, with leaves (Tuia could not understand him) approached slowly to an extremely angry Gabrys.

With the head down, one could hardly recognize the features of a little boy, all green, thin, but very agile by the way he jumped off the big tree.

"It wasn't me; I just saw the beautiful Tuia." The little leaf elf turned to look at Tuia and winked at her. "Then I was so excited by her arrival, that I really had to tell someone and confided in my friend Magnolia, then we were heard by a hawk, a hoopoe, some sparrows and … Ah yes, the tortoise, that ugly tortoise, it is so quick to spread the news."

Tuia chuckled. If it hadn't been for the gravity of the moment, it would have been a really comical scene, but Abeius freeze her instantly with his stern gaze.

"Rosewood shut up!" Gabrys immediately called him back, but the leaf elf had already gone to Tuia, curious to see her up close;

the witch looked up at the sky, exasperated. Then, speaking in a despondent tone to General Salix, she said: "Very well General, then take us to the king."

Tuia, Abeius and Gabrys were invited to follow the delegation of the soldiers of King Anax. When they started to walk towards the horses that would take them to the palace, Gabrys noticed that the leaf elf followed them, as he was going for a walk.

"Where are you going, Rosewood? You have not been invited." Gabrys rebuked him irritated.

"Can I have the honour of accompanying the young Tuia and maybe tell her a little about the valley, customs, habits and politics of the place?" Rosewood spoke pompously and almost ironically; he knew how to annoy the witch and it amused him.

"Obviously, you know enough about everything and everyone. Eh, nosy little guy?" Gabrys was furious.

"I am informed about everything. I work to make the valley flourish, for the majesty of the trees, for the growth of flowers with my friend Magnolia … I am a leaf elf at the end. Then look around … it is clear that I do my job very well and often taking care of all the places of the kingdom, listening, in spite of myself, to what people say and I see what is happening around."

So saying the leaf elf turned to Tuia and Abeius and made a sumptuous bow.

"Ok, okay, I'll introduce you to the most educated elf in the valley," Gabrys said, twisting her nose as they climbed onto the horses that would take them to the castle.

Abeius and Tuia had climbed on a magnificent white horse, while Gabrys mounted a stallion of a bright, proud and beautiful black. Rosewood took advantage of the distraction of the witch who admired her steed to jump behind her.

Gabrys turned abruptly and the leaf elf presented her his beautiful, arrogant smile at two thousand teeth.

"You won, but do me a favour: shut up." The witch surrendered.

"Very beautiful!"

Rosewood rejoiced as if he were going to the village festival. Anaktoron, the king's grand palace, towered over the sunny, colorful and cheerful valley, but there was no joy in Abeius's heart that he already knew what he was going towards.

Chapter XI

The high sun was beating over the valley, Tuia was ravished by all that beauty: the kingdom of Pantalica and the fascinating panorama that could be seen from the hill brightened her soul and made her proud of her Island. The horseback ride beside Abeius continued pleasantly until a huge shadow enveloped them: it was that of the great Anaktoron, the manor of King Anax.

The horses entered a farmyard and General Salix dismounted followed by all the others, including Tuia who was helped by Abeius. Rosewood jumped somersaulted and came down as he was flying while Gabrys had some difficulty due to her long black lace dress.

"The king is waiting for us." General Salix turned to Abeius who went ahead with him, followed by Tuia, Gabrys and Rosewood.

The doors opened. The throne room was magnificent with tall white columns that seemed to touch the sky, vases full of flowers and everywhere a soft light like that reflected by a river; in front of the entrance door a throne with a rather elderly person sitting, serious.

Gabrys took Tuia's hand and grabbed Rosewood by the arm and slowed down, detaching herself a couple of meters from the two generals, who were proud to go to King Anax.

Arriving a few meters from the throne, General Salix spoke: "Your Majesty King Anax, I brought you General Abeius of the Green Valley of Alcantara, as you requested."

It was a moment, the king got up quickly from the throne, drawing his sword, throwing himself at Abeius who had meanwhile extracted his. "Now you will die like my wife and my daughters! What revenge it is!" shouted the king with bloodshot eyes and bared teeth, like a beast eager to kill, turning his face into that of a hellish monster.

Nothing was faster than Salix and his soldiers to block the killing spree of the king against Abeius who was already ready to defend himself.

"No elf will ever kill another elf, much less can the king afford to kill a guardian of the earth. King Anax, revenge, resentment and hatred do not belong to us, cloud the mind and destroy the heart. We are not as weak as men, we are elves. We exist to give life to nature, only with good feelings is this possible.

Put down your trusty sword and talk to this general who came to you today … there is a wind of change and this is always favorable."

Tuia had remained petrified, afraid of that scene. Gabrys after the words of General Salix took her, taking her to a secondary room quickly, next to the throne room.

The king was motionless, he seemed to have become small. He fell to his knees, his legs succumbed to the emotional weight of that attack of anger. He was crying and stone tears fell on his face. He hadn't cried since he had sworn revenge and now his petrified heart was crumbling.

General Salix took an arm of his beloved king and when he lifted him from the ground, he no longer saw an old man, but the rejuvenated and valiant face of an elf: the wrinkles had disappeared and the shadows of his eyes had left two immense blue skies.

"I will be grateful to you forever, my dear general, my friend. Never an elf will hit another elf, not even the king … Thanks for having freed me from hatred and the heavy shadow that obscured my eyes, now I can see reality and see life again."

"King Anax is enormously sorry for what happened to your family. I was destined to do what I did, but I know for sure that your queen and your daughters are alive in the great volcano, the Palics revealed it to me in a dream and I will free them from the dragon." Abeius had knelt to the king of Pantalica and revealed what the twins had revealed to him in a tormented dream several decades earlier.

At that news the king again began to cry, this time tears of joy, he embraced Abeius and continued to cry for some time.

Meanwhile, Tuia, inside the enormous and sumptuous room where the witch had brought her, wanted to know why King Anax was so determined to hit Abeius. Gabrys, in a corner, recounted what she knew and that is that Abeius had stolen Tuia from the dragon Typhoeus who then, furious, had hurled himself against the elven people and kidnapped the king's wife and daughters.

"So, I am the cause of all this! Why? Abeius didn't have to do it!"

Tuia started going back and forth in the increasingly angry room. Instantly her hair became inflamed, the flames of the candles broke away and at first, they floated in the air, then they began to flutter fast like flaming arrows.

Gabrys threw himself to the ground shouting to Tuia to calm herself, but the young woman was prey to an attack of anger and her emotions had caused fire and flames everywhere, the room had become a furnace, it looked like the eruption of a volcano.

Gabrys grabbed Tuia by the legs, threw her to the ground and put a hand on her heart.

Everything calmed down suddenly, Tuia's hair returned to normal and all the flames around the room went out. The smell of burning filled the air as the elf returned conscious. Lying on the cold marble, she began to cry silently.

Gabrys called two elves of the palace to help her lift Tuia and take her to the crystal room. Gently Tuia was taken by delicate but strong arms that led her to the east wing of the castle. They entered through a very small door, where only one at a time could be accessed, but that narrow entrance opened into an immense luminous hall, where there was a blue cascade of warm water and a small pond from which the steam rose slightly.

Tuia was placed on the edge of the pool by the king's two elves, Gabrys came close and lovingly whispered to her: "This is a magic room, the crystal room. Take a relaxing bath, these waters will help you calm down."

Gabrys left, leaving the young elf alone. Tuia slowly entered the water and felt relief, calmed down a bit but always thought of

Abeius. The walls of that place were crystal blue and she stared at herself in their reflection, while white linen curtains came down from the ceiling, she thought she seemed to be inside a dream.

The witch in the meantime was running in the throne room because she had to warn Abeius as soon as possible of what had happened in Tuia a few minutes before.

"Oh, my dear friend, my bat ... Gabrys is a great pleasure to see you."

The king was smiling as never before and motioned for Gabrys to come forward. "Then you are the witch of the curse told so much" said Abeius turning to stare her intently.

"Thank you, your majesty, it is also an honor for me to meet you and see that you are better."

Gabrys was relieved to see that the king had returned to be the authoritative and attentive person she knew. Then she turned to General Abeius: "My name is Gabrys, the bat, and yes, I am the witch who carried the Triskelion when that damned dragon destroyed it. I came from a northern island, to save this island from the hatred and wars of the peoples who wanted to conquer it, but the dragon Typhoeus mistook us for enemies and attacked us, destroying the amulet and the seed of genesis and thus giving life to the curse of eternal sterility. Now Abeius let's not talk about this because I have something to tell you, the last news of your young elf."

Gabrys spoke very quickly anxious to dismiss Abeius from the king as soon as possible when a scream pierced the air.

"It's she!"

Abeius drew his sword and ran to the place from where he had heard Tuia scream, quickly opened the small door, struggling to enter due to the width of his shoulders and he entered frightened into the crystal room, wherein the midst of the enormous luminous hall, motionless, there was a naked Tuia which was reflected upset in the blue crystal walls. Gabrys came running behind Abeius, grabbed him by the shoulders and threw him out of the room, then quickly took a light linen cloth and gave it to

Tuia to cover herself.

"What is it, what happened to you, my damned soul?"

Tuia discovered her breast and showed the witch the imprint of a dragon's paw and with tears in her eyes said to her: "Burn! I belong to the dragon, right? This is his touch and I know for sure that I am a guardian of fire." Tuia spoke and sobbed.

"I want to talk to Abeius …"

Gabrys called him and Abeius opened the door; he had laid down his sword and looked troubled. The witch came out of the crystal room, knew it was time for the general to clear Tuia's doubts.

The young elf sat on the edge of the blue pond and stared at the waterfall that gushed out in front of her. Abeius immediately understood that she was very upset and let her decide to speak. He sat down next to her and remained for a while looking at her in silence, beautiful in the reflection of the waters.

"Abeius, I belong to the dragon, to the fire. You had no right to kidnap me causing all those tragedies. Now I know that my element is fire, I will learn to control it, but you have to bring me back … He suffers, I saw him, I dreamed him the other night when we arrived in Gabrys. "… Tuia was no longer crying. She finished speaking, turned to look at Abeius, and stared at him with a questioning look.

After a moment of reflection, after having looked at her intently in the large green eyes, moist but firm, the general understood that it was time for Tuia to know.

"Tuia you were destined for me from the beginning. You wear a small pinecone around your neck, that gift that a fir tree gave you … that is the seed of Genesis, you had it in your left hand when I took you away from the dragon. The stars have given us hope with your arrival, but the seed of Genesis can only be planted and grown by a guardian of the earth, that is, by someone like me. Do you understand now? Believe me, an elf doesn't steal, he doesn't betray, and he keeps his promises and mine is to protect you, always. I'll take you back to the dragon if that's what you want."

"That's what I want, general. Now the king is waiting for me, it is better that I go to make me presentable."

Tuia wrapped herself in a white linen cloth and went to the next room where the two elves had arranged some clothes, leaving Abeius alone and thoughtful.

Chapter XII

In another kingdom the sun no longer shone for some time, the fumes of Etna obscured it with perennial clouds making the great manor on Mount Tauro, even darker and darker. Here was the powerful king Adranos, passed to the dark forces to rule an army of black men and monsters, generated by his own wickedness, by too much greed, presumption and by the desire to command over everything and everyone.

The king ruled alone on a throne of terror surrounded by his monstrous dogs, the Branchiere dogs, molossers that seemed nourished with poison so much they were dangerous and angry. The emblem of his family was precisely the head of this dog, in blood-red, which sprouted menacingly from the armor of his men.

The Sicels were always accompanied by their dogs, they bred a molosser species native to the Trinacria, to which they attributed a spiritual image of protection, friendship and loyalty; the branchiere was their most faithful ally, but also their servant, a guardian who was used to punish those who committed crimes; the king had surrounded himself with these trustworthy animals, subtracting them even by force from the peasant families and then training them at his will.

Adranos had made these dogs a warrior race, in fact, he used them as war dogs, he threw them to attack (several hundred specimens) as breakthrough cavalry. Difficult to hit with arrows and javelins, they managed to unseat enemy knights by biting their horses at the hocks or attacking them from behind, like lions.

They were also able to hunt down the fugitives, and the Sicel king often used them to control his borders against the Sicans invasions. Adranos burned with the desire to command the whole island and waited for the right moment to attack and eliminate once and for all the elves who ruled the territories made inaccessible by their invincible armies, but, in particular, by unassailable protection spells. He cursed the day he had let the little elf go and now he ardently wanted to possess her, exploit her power … A Greener in his hands would have meant commanding an element that would have made him more powerful, more monstrous.

When he realized he had lost the only way to be truly invincible, the fear of losing the battle against the Phoenician invaders had led him to look for the dark side going from sea monsters to make diabolical pacts with them: they would have commanded with him the Sicel people, protected the king and fought for him against the conquerors and against the elves.

He and they would have reigned on the whole island with a powerful and horrendous army.

In exchange for immortality, he had promised his wife's life, Queen Thalia, as a sacrifice to the sea monsters Ceto and Phorcys, but he had not found her. She was gone, surely helped by her elf friends … But he would have found her one day, and he would have wetted and sealed that inhuman pact with her blood.

The kingdom of King Adranos already included half the island, from Cape Pelorus to Cape Pachynum up to the Hymera river. Moreover, he had deployed his hideous armies against the Sicans and the Elymians, peoples who lived in the western part of the island.

The only drawback in his empire, the kingdoms of Pantalica and Alcantara where the elves lived.

"Majesty, the young elf is back."

Suddenly a black soldier appeared in the throne room, with a grin on his face, and he knew how much the king expected that news.

A chilling laugh reverberated between those lava stone walls. King Adranos, laughing but without cheer, only leaked evil, so much so that even his messenger was afraid of it.

"Where is she, when did she arrive?"

"The sea monsters Ceto and Phorcys are waiting for you on the south coast of Naxos, they want to talk to you about this event."

The black-armored soldier bowed and left quickly, pleased to say goodbye to his king, who in a moment had transfigured himself into a fierce madness.

The king Adranos, excited by the fortunate news, shouted: "Prepare my horse, I will go alone to the coast to meet those horrible monsters."

After five minutes, the Sicels king galloped down towards the coast of Naxos to meet Ceto and Phorcys.

The strong wind swelled the dark waves of the Ionius sea that bathed the eastern coasts of the island, the air was unbearable because it was so hot but this did not prevent the king from arriving early on the rock where he could see monstrous figures emerging from the water, were Ceto and Phorcys, with the horrible daughters Scylla, Echidna and Ladon, waiting for the king of the Sicels Adranos.

"Adranos! Shouted Ceto, the most bloodthirsty, the mother of monsters. Look what present your child has given me."

Ceto showed Adranos the limb that Abeius had amputated. Then with a grin, she opened one of her other three arms and showed him a ball of green light.

"What is that?"

Adranos was a little afraid at the sight of that horrible rabble, but he showed himself imperious and contemptible. Now he was intrigued by what Ceto was showing him.

"This, my dear, is a present we made ourselves. The small human Tuia walked near a portal in a world unknown to us, and I wanted to capture and bring her here, but I failed, I could only take out her mind. The portal reopened where she really was, here on the island, but while I grabbed her that damned elf, the general of the hawks, he sliced a limb at me."

The angry monster began to scream in irritation and the other monsters did the same, making the ground and the whole coast tremble, the king had to cover his ears with those shrill screams until they ceased. "Where is she now?"

A little shaken, King Adranos wanted as much news as possible, his moment of revenge had arrived.

"In the kingdom of Pantalica, under King Anax." The deformed Phorcys, Ceto's husband, replied with a grin to King Adranos; he knew the black king hated the elves.

King Adranos was furious and organized a plan to move immediately and cruelly.

"This is the time to act, Scylla, you will go to Cape Pelorus where you will find Charybdis. Your thirst for blood is about to be satisfied: you will have to be ruthless; will not have to pass any ships from the Strait.

Echidna and Ladon, you will go west by land, the other by sea. You will bring terror and death on the Sicans and the Elymians, it is time they leave their territories to me.

Ceto and Phorcys we will take care of our guests: it is time for the elves to know who is in charge here. They will try to save the humans and we will wait for them with open arms … Ceto you will succeed with the other remaining limbs to strangle that cursed of Abeius."

At those words the monsters screamed again excitedly, spraying and raising the violent sea waves that hit the coastal area, then the sea monsters sank: Scylla swam towards Cape Pelorus to meet the mortal Charybdis to terrorize the coasts to the north the island, Echidna and Ladon also left for their bloody mission and Phorcys and Ceto returned to their dark submarine meanders bringing with them the luminous green sphere.

From a far corner of the abysses, another sea creature had followed all the events and tried to understand the intentions of the brothers Ceto and Phorcys, it was the old and wise Nereus.

Unlike his siblings, Nereus was not an evil monster, he was a wise old man who could take on different appearances, like those of a sea snake or turn into a cold fire; he foresaw the future and his marine kingdom was in the Aegean Sea, but evil waves had accompanied him curiously near the eastern coasts of Trinacria to peek at the misdeeds of relatives.

He had understood what the brothers intended to do, but he

wouldn't allow it: he was a guardian himself and he would have warned the young Tuia, he would have tried to steal the green sphere from the clutches of Ceto and Phorcys, he would … but how?

Nereus and his wife Doride had fifty daughters called Nereids, lived in the depths of the sea with their father and often helped sailors and travellers in difficulty, rode dolphins and other marine animals. The old Nereus gave himself no peace, he still had to do something and wanted advice, he summoned his daughters and explained the bad situation to them.

"Poor little Greener …" all the young Nereids exclaimed in chorus. They were upset and one of them, the shrewdest and bravest, Galateia, proposed: "I'll take the ball for you father, but it will have to be hidden in a place where only the last-born elf can retrieve it, we can't risk losing it for a second time."

Nereus was proud of his daughter Galateia and knew she was right, he had to consult the oracle of the sea to be sure about how to act.

He swam to Cape Lilybaeum, accompanied by killer whales and dolphins, his marine army and at midnight came to the Cathedral cave, where the moonlight would awaken the oracle, the important Mediterranean voice.

At a depth of about thirty meters, there was a very large cavity, like a royal hall, colonnaded by gleaming stalactites and stalagmites, a sandy bottom wherein the center there was the majestic oracle's column.

Nereus came alone into the underwater cave: it was no place for anyone, only the guardians could enter it without being electrocuted. He went in silent, with his right hand and with his left touched the tip of the stalagmites placed on the sides of the entrance and the moonlight spread from stalagmite to stalagmite, the crystals lit up like tall lamps, radiated in a circle until they went to end in the central column which was illuminated by a dazzling light.

"Nereus, wise of the sea, speak, the Oracle of the Cathedral Cave is awake. What do you want to know?"

A female voice boomed in the sea cave; the oracle had awoken from the submarine sleep.

"The precious thoughts of a child have been stolen by my brothers, the sea monsters Ceto and Phorcys."

Nereus spoke with fear and reverence, it was always a great honor for him to hear the oracle.

"Of course… the kid in question is the human part of Tuia, the last-born elf, you can talk openly …"

"How and where can I safely hide the green sphere of thoughts? I can't touch her because she is a guardian of fire and me of water … I could damage her." Said Nereus, worried, always feeling undeserving of listening to the oracle.

"Ahahahah, when the prophecies concern you, you don't see them, well! Listen, wise Nereus, I will speak only once … There is a hidden head, dangerous and with a deadly look, where snakes still live because they are immortal and reinforced by petrifying eyes. It is protected by the sisters Stheno and Euryale. Give them the precious thoughts, no one will ever dare to touch her, not even the unworthy mother. Only Tuia will one day have her assets back, only her. "After these words, the Cathedral Cave returned to being dark. Nereus waited, hoping that the Oracle would return to speak but he knew that it was all over, after all from an oracle he could not expect clarity.

"The head of Medusa, how and who …"

Thoughtfully Nereus came out of the cave and reached his waiting marine army, and he continued to brood on the way back.

Returning to the Ionius sea, the sage Nereus was welcomed by his forty-nine daughters relieved to see him arrive. The fiftieth was gloating sitting with a bright green sphere in her hand, she was the smiling and brave Galateia returning victorious from her dangerous mission.

"Here it is, father. It was an easy job: Phorcys likes sleeping, your brothers don't shine much for intelligence, Ceto will kill him for this."

"Galateia you were very brave and cunning. "And while he was talking, an idea came up to Nereus.

"Come with me, dear, but hide the sphere in your seaweed bag."

The two swam together towards the shore of Naxos beach and Nereus told what the oracle had predicted.

A horse was waiting for them on the beach.

"Now my daughter, trust it, will know where to go. When you arrive at your destination you will find a small temple, in Selinos, where the head of Medusa lies."

At the words of her father Galateia had a shock.

"Don't be afraid. At the entrance of the Temple, you will find the Graeae, blinds their only eye with a little dust, then without wasting time you run inside and hand over the ball to the Gorgons, no one will ever dare go and take it there, not even Ceto and Phorcys: Medusa is mortal for them too, ungrateful parents who did nothing to save her. After, throwing yourself into the sea and swim as fast as you can. Return safe and sound, my daughter."

Nothing replied Galateia, climbed on the horse that awaited her and galloped off into the night, under the faint light of the moon, meanwhile in the sky, the Perseids shone as never before indicating the path to the daring Nereid.

Chapter XIII

"Here we are, now I will meet the king … What will I do? What will I tell him? I'm the cause of his ills … I'm so nervous … Damn you, Abeius."

Tuia went to the throne room and brooded like a grinder. Leaving her room, she had taken the arm offered by Rosewood, ignoring that of Abeius, to be accompanied by the king in an elegant peach-colored long dress.

"Here you are, at last, I have waited so long to meet you, dear." King Anax smiled at an anxious and tense Tuia who succeeded only to make a rather clumsy bow.

"Majesty, she is Tuia Orientalis, the beautiful, splendid, wonderful …"

"ROSEWOOD!" shouted Gabrys angrily. "Sweet elf … and General Abeius. Well, you know him already!" With a sumptuous reverence, Rosewood stepped aside and showed Abeius behind him.

Gabrys snorted in laughter, after noticing that Abeius's face claimed he wanted to strangle the leaf elf.

"Majesty, I wanted to tell you I'm sorry …"

Tuia had begun to speak almost in tears but was blocked by King Anax.

"Dear, my daughters and my wife are alive, your general has promised to bring them back to me. We no longer think about this story, we have other things to worry about."

Tuia turned to look at Abeius, who nodded his head with a slight smile, she looked at him gratefully and simply murmured: "Thank you."

A regal and rich banquet awaited them: the best fruits of the earth, abundant milk and honey and then fruit salads and many glazed pancakes, they never ended, marvelous to the eyes and the palate.

“Rosewood, join us,” said Tuia, showing him the delicacies of the table.

“Oh no, no, leaf elves don’t need to eat. On the contrary, I leave you and this wonderful company and go back to work … The vegetation needs me, the day has been torrid and tonight nature needs to be refreshed. Dear Tuia, see you soon, enjoy your dinner. As you can see, it’s all my work …”

“But how pompous you are, go away, before I leaf you through.” So, saying the witch made the leaf elf escape, which, as at his usual, he made a somersault and one of his sumptuous bows and disappeared.

Everyone smiled, the air was finally more relaxed and Tuia realized she had the most special person in the world next to her and that she would never doubt her General Abeius again.

At the end of the evening the speeches became more serious, King Anax told Abeius how Adranos, the king of the Sicels, had betrayed the elves and that now reigned supreme the whole eastern part of the island with sea monsters as allies.

Tuia became nervous again: the kingdom of Adranos was under the volcano and she had to reach the dragon.

Abeius understood what was on her mind.

“Majesty, Tuia needs to learn to use the bow and the sword: our journey on the Etna will be difficult and she must know how to defend herself. I ask you to host us so that I can give her lessons personally.”

“General you will have my armories and training spaces available. Make her a warrior, we trust in her, the whole island trusts in her.”

“Thank you, your majesty, we won’t disappoint you.”

Abeius put the fingers of his left hand on his mouth and then on his heart as a sign of promise.

Tuia was already thinking about the sword that Abeius possessed and that she couldn’t even lift, she was curious to try a bow too, but she was frightened for those workouts she already imagined were long and tiring.

"Nice night majesty, we take our leave. Tomorrow morning, we will start training very soon."

Abeius accompanied Tuia to her room, the day was full of emotions and the following day training would be hard: they had to rest and clear their mind a bit to face a new day.

From the windows of her room, Tuia could see the stars. She loved looking at them and trying to recognize them by their size and brightness. She recognized almost all the constellations but one for her was new or maybe she didn't recognize it.

"Gabrys, those stars that form a strange figure what are they? I don't remember ever seeing them before."

Gabrys, half asleep, went to the window to see. "Oh, it's the constellation of the dragon. Those stars had been extinguished for a while, but your arrival rekindled them: it is a sign of hope …Now you sleep. Tomorrow your day will be hard and please … Don't wake me up anymore."

Gabrys went back to sleep in the bed next to Tuia's who fell asleep happily watching what she thought were her stars.

It was barely dawning and already Tuia was sitting on her bed, waiting for Abeius for her first day of training.

The general was not long in coming and as soon as the sun rose, he knocked on Tuia's bedroom door, which quietly came out trying not to wake Gabrys.

"Forgive me, I will never doubt you again."

Abeius with his kind smile simply replied:

"Good morning, dear."

Tuia was quieter now and would face everything with her general by her side. They went down into a stone courtyard against the high walls and there a rack of swords of all kinds awaited them.

"Put these on."

Abeius handed Tuia a leather bodice, handguards, and knee pads, then showed her the swords.

“There are different types of swords, see this longer and bigger one called” bastard “or one-and-a-half sword, it can be used with one hand or two, it is a sword that comes from our northernmost lands. Here there is a short sword and this one instead a long sword, this other is a two-handed sword, but you will start with a lighter one: a short sword, here take it!”

Tuia tried to grab Abeius’s sword from the hilt but missed it and fell noisily to the ground. A laugh was heard on her head, when the disgruntled elf raised the head to look up, she noticed that perched on a high branch of a large poplar, there was a figure all covered with roses petals that looked like a child.

“Hi, I’m Magnolia. From your surprise, I assume you have never seen a petal elf. Sorry if I laughed but you had such a funny face. Don’t be afraid, try and try again, you’ll learn soon. You are an elf, remember that.”

“Pleased to meet you. Rosewood told me about you, work together, if so you can say.”

As she spoke Tuia picked up the sword from the ground but did not look away from the strange and delicate little person.

“Yeah, but I haven’t seen him since tonight. He was on the coast: the prickly pears must have begun to bear fruit, but apparently, he found something more interesting to do.”

“What?” Tuia asked, curious to hear something more from that lovely creature, who smelled of orange blossom and roses.

“Well, I saw him follow a damsel on horseback. Actually, I had never seen that girl in those parts, and I think she was in a hurry.”

“Should we still have a conversation or can we start training?”

Abeius with folded arms was impatient to start the lesson but, in the meantime, he was amused by the way Tuia was looking at the petal elf, who at that moment smelled of lavender.

The day was heavy. Tuia trained incessantly, determined to block at least one of Abeius’s lunges, instead of running away when he attacked her. And so, after many and many attempts at defense, in the light of sunset Tuia finally succeeded in stopping a shot from Abeius and launching an attack as if in her life she had done nothing but fight with the sword.

"Strike! Bring out your elven nature and fight! Don't be afraid to hurt me, look inside yourself and you will find all the strength you need."

The two practiced until late at night until they, exhausted, they lay down on the ground.

The sky was starry, the stars shone like never had before. "Abeius those are my stars, do you know it? It's the constellation of the dragon, Gabrys told me last night about it."

"Yes, you come from there, you are the daughter of the fire of the stars. A meteor brought you to us. Everything you are will come out and you will be able to overcome anything when you discover yourself, nothing will seem impossible to you."

"But I feel so small compared to all this."

"Take strength from nature Tuia, nature never disappoints, it is loyal, generous and powerful. That curse has tried to stop the natural cycle of genesis, but you have come to us to free us … how? We are not able to know, but your instinct will guide you."

"So, come to dinner or do we want to set up a banquet under the stars?" Gabrys had appeared smiling. She clapped her hands a couple of times and elves carried tables and benches in the courtyard, under that wonderful starry sky. Tuia and Abeius, surprised by the appearance of Gabrys, stood up abruptly and a little uncomfortably ran into their rooms to make themselves presentable for the banquet under the stars.

Songs and dances, along with the traditional tarantellas, were played all evening and Tuia danced a lot, serene and amused. The elves competed for those who had to dance with her, beautiful elves circled her, graceful in their light clothes, like pink, lilac, yellow and blue flowers, in their dance they almost seemed to hover in the air like butterflies.

Only an elf didn't dance. General Abeius observed the dances from afar and stood to stare at Tuia, glad she enjoyed herself.

Suddenly he remembered the Palics, the fortune-tellers he had met in a dream in his distant past. The memory blurred his vision, but their words still echoed inside his head: "Your consort will come from the stars and you will grow up her with awareness of her being, with paternal love, you will defend her at the risk of your own life until that day will come."

A premonitory dream that was overwhelming often resurfaced to upset him. Abeius was shocked by that memory and thought of the young Tuia, of his time with her. He had seen her grow up, but he would never have revealed anything. He turned and started back into the large dining room as Tuia began to dance with General Salix. That dance lasted all evening: the beautiful elf was an excellent dancer and taught Tuia many new dances, especially the traditional and ancient dances of the island.

Abeius sat gloomily in a corner of the dining room from where he could see the outside of the courtyard, watching Tuia, enchanting in her light white dress, dancing with Salix. That situation was starting to bother him a bit: he was a little jealous, even if he didn't want to admit it to himself.

Gabrys followed the whole evening, watching with her watchful eye the behavior of everyone, especially Tuia, struck by the gentle manner of the elegant general Salix. For his part, the general of the hawthorn did not disdain the company of the young elf and it was clear that the dance had awakened a sweet feeling in both.

Having also noticed Abeius, sitting alone inside the castle, so Gabrys went to sit beside him.

"What a beautiful evening!" The witch tried to break the ice but received only a grunt from Abeius.

"Look at how the little girl enjoys herself … You could go and dance a little too."

"I don't dance, in fact now it's time to end this" beautiful "evening … Tuia must rest, tomorrow she will have other training sessions."

"Ah yes, of course, tomorrow bow will be her weapon … Salix will be her teacher, isn't he?"

"Whoever he is, I'll be there with her. Goodnight."

And Gabrys smiled at these new little love problems. As Abeius accompanied Tuia to her room, he noticed that she was still excited by the evening.

"Abeius, but Salix, oops, how old is General Salix?"

"Enough," Abeius replied dryly, somewhat annoyed.

"But what age am I here, am I small?"

Abeius stopped and realized he had to explain something to her.

"So Tuia, here, you are a young elf, adult but young. Salix and I are adult elves. As you may have noticed, there are no old people, an elf grows over the centuries, but he never grows old because if this happened, all of nature would die … We don't count our age, we don't need it, but what is useful is to use our time to the fullest possible, avoiding ugliness and malice."

Tuia looked down thoughtfully and:

"Goodnight my friend." The dreamy young elf smiled and closed the door behind her.

"By the way, you're small for Salix, if you want to know!" He would have liked to scream behind her but remained silent, thoughtful, looking at the void.

Tuia was still dancing inside herself in the memory of that magical evening with the sky-colored eyes of her general Salix imprinted on her eyes.

Gloomy Abeius went for a walk around the castle and stopped in front of the open door of the armory where he saw Salix arranging bows and arrows for the next day.

"Come on, man, something upsets you? You were very skilled today with the sword. I saw you; you know her! You managed to take her on her way with great skill. You understand her, you understand its being and you know how to manage it … Maybe because you're a Guardian like her?"

Salix spoke without looking up from the quivers he was filling with arrows, meticulously checking them one by one.

"I don't understand her, I know her. She has been with me since she was born, and I am bound to her by a promise to live."

"And from love."

Salix looked up to stare at Abeius. "You can't deny it, I can even read your fear of me in your face. Brother, know that if she were to choose me and my heart should accept her, she will never be in danger, for what she represents for our world and for what she will be for me."

Abeius did not answer, he merely said bye with his head and left, this time in his room to avoid other night meetings. He didn't really want to talk to anyone.

Chapter XIV

"Ah! Today I have the training with Salix! It can't be, I don't feel ready … How am I doing?"

Abeius had just touched the door of Tuia's room that she went out like a fury, more agitated than ever.

"Good morning, baby, you will train with General Salix today, and I will be there with you … However, you are dressed well, and very pretty."

He wanted to say to her: "Take off that lipstick," but restrained that little leap of jealousy, he had to try to regulate himself and not give in to what was a bad feeling.

Tuia pawed. She wanted to start training immediately, she wanted to see immediately the beautiful general of the hawthorn.

As soon as they went out into the courtyard, the morning sun dazzled them, but the young elf did nothing but smile at the beautiful master archer who was waiting for her, shining in the sun, in white dressed. His blond hair glistened like gold and his blue eyes made even the morning blue sky look gloomy.

"Hello, dear friends, did you sleep well?" Today we will start our lesson knowing the bows."

"Good morning, Salix. If I don't disturb you, I would like to go there to follow the training."

Abeius settled on a beautiful bench in finely carved stone with a hawthorn engraved in the center.

"Abeius please sit down. The elves of the hawthorn are the most skilled and competent with the bow, without taking away from the elves of King Corylus masters of the sword."

Salix was radiant and also proud to have the honor of teaching the last-born elf while Tuia began to feel a little uncomfortable with the fact that she had never held a bow in her hand … And moreover, it would have been the general Salix to teach her how to do it!

But she didn't say anything, her mouth had also dried up.

"Well let's start. As you can see, we can have bows of different types, hunting, and battle bows. We are elves and we will never go hunting, we hate hunting: never an elf will kill another living being, at this point, this will be our bow."

Salix turned and took a rather long wooden bow that looked light and was finely inlaid.

"This is a Longbow or long bow, it is a battle weapon that has ancient origins, the elves use it to defend themselves from attacks, but they don't want and create war ever, remember Tuia."

Tuia nodded almost hypnotized by Salix's elegant way of explaining and followed each word carefully.

"This bow is built with yew tree wood or the tree of death. With this you can't go wrong: you aim and throw the arrow, I'll show you."

At the end of the courtyard, very, very far away, a mannequin had been placed, Salix quickly extended the bow and threw the arrow that struck the heart of the straw man.

"Splendid and terrible," Tuia thought, fascinated by the power of that bow, then cheered happily at Salix's performance before turning to Abeius who pretended to clap with a forced smile.

"Now it's your turn Tuia."

Tuia approached Salix, he followed her and took her hands placing them on the bow and with one hand he nocked the arrow. Tuia blushed: she couldn't concentrate on the mannequin at the bottom of the courtyard, she could only smell Salix, his hair brushing her face and his hands clutching her own.

Now the general made her stretch the bow. What strength he had in his arms … she just couldn't take her mind off the fact that he had wonderful and muscular arms.

Now the arrow shot. Tuia had a fleeting vision of the dart that was thrown and suddenly caught fire, hitting the mannequin that was incinerated in an instant.

"What happened? Excuse me, it didn't have to happen … What a shame, what a shame …"

The young elf didn't give herself peace, she almost had tears in her eyes. Abeius got up quickly and ran to calm her, putting aside Salix who tried to explain to her that nothing serious had happened, he hugged her and took her to sit on the bench.

It seemed that Tuia had suffered almost a shock, Abeius tried to talk to her but she always said that it should not happen.

"Well, my little girl needs a nice relaxing potion." Gabrys suddenly appeared with a large crystal glass with a steaming yellow drink.

Tuia ran to meet her as soon as she saw her and thanking her drank the potion the witch had prepared for her in one breath. "Gabrys thank you very much, really." Tuia had returned a slight smile and her pale face began to regain its color.

Gabrys took Abeius by the arm and sat him back on the stone bench. The general stared at her insistently.

"I figured it could happen. Nothing that could not be solved with a bit of psychology and a good dose of chamomile." The witch turned and winked at Abeius.

In the meantime, the burned mannequin was replaced with another intact and Tuia resumed training.

A little more relaxed, she began to follow the movements of her teacher and she enjoyed the moments when he took her arms and touched her cheeks with his delicately perfumed face, moments that instilled peace and serenity.

At the end of that long, hard and tiring day of training, Tuia had already learned well enough to shoot with bow and Abeius was very proud of her.

The young elf was now cooked, lost in love with General Salix, one of those cooked in which one has no eyes but for him, eyes that in this case were two immense oceans to dive into.

While they returned tired and satisfied to the castle an elf ran towards them and turned to Salix urging to follow him. The general apologized and ran away leaving Tuia, Abeius, and Gabrys to wonder what had happened so alarmingly.

When they reached the entrance courtyard, they noticed horses and soldiers returning from their reconnaissance lap, and between them, they noticed an exhausted horse with a man over fainted, a human being. The elves had not taken care of men for a long time, but perhaps things were changing.

"General Salix is a Sican. We found him on the eastern bank of the Hymera River and he called for help desperately."

The soldier showed the battered man passed out on the saddle of his horse, battered and tired too.

"Take him to the healers, arrange and refresh his horse. I will go to warn the king and then we will listen to him."

The tough attitude had given way to compassion on General Salix's face who immediately ran to King Anax. Abeius closely observed the poor man and noticed large cuts, the work of monstrous claws, and that the wounds had a bad dark color, a slimy and black substance that infected them.

Gabrys immediately realized what had happened, she told Tuia to go to her room and Abeius not to leave her for a second, she followed Salix instead.

"King Anax a stranger was found by our men on reconnaissance, not beyond our borders, on the eastern shore of Hymera river. He is a Sican, in very bad condition. The healers are giving him first aid."

Salix was anxious about the reaction of the king who was already beginning to change his mood and seem annoyed.

"A man in my kingdom? I don't want traitors here!" King Anax shouted his disapproval but his general had already foreseen such a reaction.

"He desperately asked for help and my compassionate men saved him … Isn't that what we are, people with good feelings?"

Salix tried with his words to awaken a compassionate spirit in

King Anax.

“Not with everyone, men are traitors …”

“Maybe not, not all … I can’t believe they are all contemptuous and bad. I ask you to be able to listen to this unfortunate stranger and understand what brought him close to our borders.” Salix looked the king in the eye, he trusted his good soul.

“Bring him here, I want to hear what he has to say.”

The king spoke gruffly, already inside he was worried about new events.

Gabrys looked at him proud to be her friend and smiled at him lovingly.

Supported by two elves, the poor man was led before the king. “Who are you human? Where did you come from and why they found you close to my borders in these conditions? Speaks!”

The king wanted to seem imperious, but at the sight of that man in such a bad condition, the pain invaded him, and his voice began to calm down and become charitable.

“My name is Vicio and I’m a Sican … Help me, please help me …”

He fell to the ground on his knees crying. “My family, my people … The monsters … Help us …”

“Monsters? What monsters?”

The king rose from his throne and went closer to that wretch. “They’re slaughtering us, I’m looking for help for me, for my people … There are armies of black men with big monstrous and bloodthirsty dogs … They are slaughtering people. I ask you for help, help all of us…”

The poor Sican fell unconscious in the center of the room, the king looked at him dismayed by the story of so much horror.

“His wounds tell the truth; he was attacked by a monster. That is black poison: the slimy sea monsters want to conquer the island and not only … You already know who the black army is, isn’t it? That bloody of Adranos, that vile traitor is determined to slaughter the peoples of the Sicans and of the Elymians who control the entire western part of the Trinacria."

Gabrys was furious, she looked at the poor man who had regained consciousness, she had to know more.

"But how did you stay alive?"

"I don't know exactly how, but the trees saved me … Their roots, they whipped the monster that was killing me and tied its claws … and I realized that there had to be an elf's hand … so I ran a lot and I found my horse that had escaped … it was badly reduced, but it brought me close to the river and then I woke up here … Please help me, help my people …"

The poor wretch, without strength in his body, slumped to the ground.

"Save his life! Let the healers do what they can!" shouted the king so his soldiers would hurry.

Gabrys turned to the worried king: "That man is dead: his wounds are now infected, the claws of sea monsters are lethal … only the firewater could save him." She stopped to think and then Gabrys spoke again:

"Rosewood … It must have been Rosewood, he saved him. But where will it be now? I hope he's not in trouble … King Anax I have to go look for him, I have to find him."

Agitated Gabrys ran to the Tuia room, she had to warn Abeius.

She knocked and as soon as the general opened the door, she took his arm and carried it out.

"Follow me. The island is under siege and you have to prepare to leave. Tuia, ready or not, must carry out her mission. We must restrain these unclean beings; destiny must be fulfilled."

As the witch spoke, she ran up the stairs to the west tower until they reached the top. It was dark by now.

Under a black sky, with open arms, Gabrys began to rotate on herself and to invoke: "Creatures of the night, loyal and ruthless, wake up and fly to the west! Look for the leaf elf for me!"

A red mist fell on the woods from which millions of bats soared that, like a huge black cloud, melted into the night flying westward.

Then she turned to Abeius: "It's time to keep the promises made. Take her to her dragon, general. We will meet again soon, Rosewood needs me."

The witch raised her arms to the sky, joined her hands and turned into the largest bat Abeius had ever seen, flew a few seconds around and then disappeared into the night.

"Good luck, my friend."

Shaken by the latest news of Gabrys, Abeius ran down the stairs and went to the throne room where Salix still argued with the king. "They want her, the monsters know she is here and they will attack you as soon as possible."

Abeius was alarmed, he knew that those horrible monsters wouldn't stop if they didn't take Tuia.

Salix stepped forward:

"We will never leave the last elf born at the mercy of those unclean beings, much less will she return to the hands of that traitor of Adranos. I will leave to defend our borders, the army will split and will settle over the Hymera river to try to help the Sican people. Sire, King Corylus will have to be informed."

Salix looked at Abeius who nodded decisively.

"Your Majesty, Tuia and I will leave tomorrow morning at dawn. Our roads divide but we will be with you in a battle against Adranos and his monstrous army: I will lead the army of the falcons of King Corylus, we will never allow the island to go into the hands of evil. The elves, united, will win. But first I have to fulfill some promises. The great volcano awaits me."

Abeius started to leave but Salix stopped him: "I'll leave tomorrow morning too; I'd like to say goodbye to her." Abeius looked at him steadily but said nothing.

Salix knew how much this "yes" had to weigh and went to Tuia's room without delay. He knocked and the young elf slowly opened, peering first, seeing the late hour. Obviously, she was surprised to see Salix at that time, there, at her.

“Hello, general Salix, why are you here?”

Tuia understood that there was something bad in the air because the general had a grim and sad face.

“Dear Tuia, I have come to greet you. Tomorrow morning, I will lead my army beyond the borders of the kingdom of King Anax; monsters besiege western populations and elves cannot remain insensitive to their cries. It has been wonderful to know you, the time spent with you is a precious memory … For a while, we walk away but, if fate wills, we will meet soon.

Elen síla lúmenn ‘omentielvo, a star shines on the hour of our meeting.”

Tuia began to cry silently and when Salix finished speaking, she closed her eyes, expecting a sweet kiss on her lips, but the general gently took her face in her hands and kissed her on the forehead, then left without turning around, leaving Tuia stunned.

She wanted to stop him, give him that kiss she so longed for, but she realized that the love she felt for him, perhaps he still could not repay her as she wanted. She cried all night.

Chapter XV

A sad scenario appeared at the departure of General Salix's troops: the sky announced rain and the winds of late August became more insistent, but Tuia thought of his farewell. At the window she could see the fermenting stables: the stablemen were refreshing the horses and adjusting the harness, battle armor of metal and silver that shone under the lightning of the sky.

The rumble of thunder mingled with the blows on Tuia's bedroom door. It was Abeius who entered slowly while the elf remained silent at the window.

"Good morning Tuia, even if the sky promises storm, we must prepare to leave. Your dragon is waiting for you and I have to fulfill the promise made to King Anax to bring his family back to him before going to the Green Valley of Alcantara to my king, he must be warned to keep ready for battle."

"The time has come, then. Your words reverberate in my head more than the din of thunder, but if it has to be like this, so it will be …"

"King Anax makes you a gift of armor made for his first child, never worn because the dragon took her away the day before her party for maturity. It is yours which honorary citizen of the kingdom of Pantalica now, can help you and protect you on this journey. The elven metal is unassailable from external blows, no arrow can pierce it."

Amazed, Tuia bowed to that splendid and shining royal armor, with silver engravings showing a stylized hawthorn. She had never seen anything like it, so precious, she was more than honored for the respect the king dedicated to her.

"I will wear it with honor."

"That's what I expect from you, honor. Never betray yourself Tuia, trust yourself, your senses, your element. Believe in yourself. It will be hard out there, a journey full of dangers awaits us, but our cardinal point is the Triskelion, don't forget it. When you think you can't make it, think that the stars have trusted you, don't disappoint them and you won't let yourself down; the elves believe in you, you think of them and you will win.

Now get ready and wear armor, soon it will be dawn and the king will come to speak to the armies. We must be there, ready to go."

Abeius came out but Tuia looked out the window again. A silver tide was forming: all the knights of the hawthorn were ready, lined up in their silvery armor, which at every flash glowed and wounded the green eyes of the elf while she held her tears. She didn't want to cry, she didn't have to, but one question ran through her mind more than any other: would she see him again?

Abeius had risen again to the tower from where Gabrys had left, thinking of the witch, he wondered if she had found Rosewood …

He scanned the sky to the north. Etna could no longer be seen, which meant that the storm was cutting down the Etna valley; but the volcano was silent. Is Typhoeus sleeping? How would the dragon react to seeing her? What would he do to her? Could there be a danger that he would try to kill her? Surely the dragon would have tried to kill him, but he could not avoid leaving.

He looked out of the tower and saw that Salix's army was deployed, the time had come. So Abeius came down from the tower and went to the room of Tuia but the door was open and the room empty. Quickly he ran into the courtyard and immediately saw her, hidden behind a column, watching Salix give orders to his soldiers.

Abeius followed her, took her hand and led her out. Across from the enormous main gate, there was a stone rise where a tapestry depicting a hawthorn loomed.

The king had just come out and stood under his symbol. Salix, Tuia, and Abeius approached and bowed to the king, all the soldiers in a single silver wave knelt.

The king raised his arms to heaven as if to embrace them all: "For a long time we let the men ruin this island, thinking of leaving them to their own affairs, of letting them destroy each other. But this is also our island and we will defend it from anyone who wants to ruin its luxuriance, its wonderful nature. We are elves and all this belongs to us. If any man of goodwill wants to join us, he will be welcome, otherwise be on your guard! Know, my children, that you will endanger yourself to protect nature.

But basically, we exist for this. May the stars protect you!"

King Anax seemed moved but with royalty, he touched his heart and bowed slightly greeting his men, who all responded together by touching the hawthorn in the center of their armor as a sign of respect. After that, the king came down from the stone platform, went to Tuia and kissed her on the forehead: "Take care of yourself daughter."

The army mounted, Salix before mounting on his white steed turned to look at Tuia. Perhaps he wanted to tell her that he returned her love, but he did not speak, he turned his horse and preceded his army with the bearers of flags before leaving at a gallop.

It had started to rain and Tuia remained watching from the great door the hawthorn's army disappear in the distance, in the rain. Abeius, with him two battle-harnessed horses with regal harnesses, came out of the stables and watched Tuia from afar.

The incessant rain came down, but he didn't mind, in his green eyes only she reflected, beautiful in her shining armor that said goodbye to another. From his remote memories, a song appeared, a song he had listened to when it was nothing more than a large tree, a majestic fir tree. Words like waves of a stormy sea rose in his throat and pinched his eyes, words of a song from another era that spoke of the fear of not being up to that enchanting creature.

And the elf then sang:

"And I take this sword across the sky
I swear I will be a rock against fire and frost.
Only at the top will I wait for the raiders
Many will come and sail the seas.
And I will never fight for compensation.
I fight for love; I will fight for this.
I am a warrior; awake when it is night
I will defend you from nightmares and sorrows
I will give you certainties against fears
to see the world beyond those hills
Fear nothing, I will be by your side
I will wipe your tears with my cloak.
Don't fear the dragon, I will stop its fire
Nothing can hit you behind this shield
I will fight strongly against all evil
And when I fall, don't despair, I'll get up for you again.
From night to day, from west to east
There will be lights of hope
And I will hug you to always give you strength."

A tear mingled with the rain and fell heavily on the ground like a wave of the sea.

Never let your ears hear the song of an elf, because the soul is anguished and the heart cries.

I amar prestar aen, han mathon ne nen, han maton ne chae in han noston ne 'wilith.

"The world has changed, I can feel it in the water, I can feel it in the ground, I can breathe it in the air."

Chapter XVI

“Little elf where are you? I saw you; I know you’re here somewhere. You can show yourself now, the monster is gone.”

Galateia cautiously stepped out of the water, looking around to make sure the danger had passed.

All around it was horrible to the eye: the Sican people who had come to defend their borders had been mowed down by Ladon, the marine monster. The trees had been uprooted and reduced to pieces, death had taken many valiant men and others remained dying on the pavement: no one could survive the deadly and poisonous claws of sea monsters. The bodies quickly decayed, and a stench of death filled the air, making it unbreathable.

“So, where are you? Oh, for a thousand jellyfish, did he die too?”

“No, no, but it didn’t take much.” The voice came from the bark of a distant tree where the elf had camouflaged himself.

“The fight was hard … I lost almost all my leaves, but for all the prickly pears, I’m alive.”

Rosewood checked to see if his thin little body had anything broken. Apart from a few missing leaves here and there and someone else a little crumpled, he could say he got off very well compared to the poor wretches who had lost their lives in that damned fight.

The leaf elf jumped down and remained open-mouthed to look at the destruction left after the battle between the monster and the Sicans. He had never seen anything like it, no one had survived, yet he had bravely fought to help the humans.

“You were very good, little elf, you saved my life. But unfortunately, you couldn’t do anything for them: Ladon is bloody and kills whoever is in front of him, you could do nothing else alone.”

Galateia had noticed that the elf was upset and in shock by the chilling scenery under their eyes.

"I am Rosewood, I am a leaf elf. I followed you from the coast of Naxos … I had never seen you around, but I know one thing, you are not an elf and you come from the sea."

"In fact, I am Galateia, one of the fifty daughters of Nereus, the sage of the sea. I have an important mission to carry out for my father, I must bring a precious thing to safety."

"Thing? Whether it is permissible to know," asked Rosewood curiously.

"I can only tell you that I have to go to Selinos from the Gorgons because they will protect it."

"Oh well! A nice safe place, the Gorgons … Of course, as lovable as a bed of pins."

Astonished and irritated, the leaf elf did not believe what he had heard from Galateia.

"Obviously, but we're a family, they won't twist a hair from me." At least this was what Galateia hoped for inside her as she looked around anxiously, searching in vain for her horse that had fled terrified at the sight of the horrible monster.

"I understand, I'll have to walk."

Resigned Galateia said goodbye to Rosewood with her hand and began to walk westward.

"Wait, I can accompany you if you want. And when you have reached your destination, I will return home knowing that you have arrived safely."

Rosewood was sure he didn't want to let her go alone and then he wanted to understand what that monster wanted from the Sican people, why all that violence?

As they walked, death and destruction filled the horizon. The little elf was more and more determined to understand who wanted all this.

Galateia, however, was absorbed in her thoughts and a faint smile came to her face when she thought of the awakening of Phorcys that he would not find the green sphere of thoughts that he had to keep. Ceto would have gone on a rampage, perhaps she would have killed him, bloody and instinctive as she was. "One less monster," the beautiful Nereid muttered to herself.

In fact, something happened in the deep and dark sea meanders. Phorcys, had he woken up from his sleep and realized that the green sphere was missing, had he lost the precious thoughts of Tuia or someone had stolen it? Should he warn Ceto or go look for it alone?

But while he was hesitant about what to do, Ceto arrived as arrogant and horrendous as ever.

"Get up miserable mischievous, we have an island to conquer and you are still there … Where is it, where did you put it?" Ceto immediately noticed that the green sphere was missing, her eyes were burning with rage and with her monstrous claws, she grabbed Phorcys by the throat, which unable to react, struggled to speak: "I don't know, I didn't find it, someone must have stolen it!"

The monster was trying to explain himself, but his sister's grip was powerful.

"Dirty, miserable little monster, we must find it immediately!"

Ceto, maddened, left her submarine cavern and with a deafening screech, she managed to raise twenty-meter- high waves that crashed on some Sicel fishing boats that were there, sinking them instantly.

Not far away, the daughters of Nereus realized that Ceto was raging for the disappearance of the sphere and ran to save the poor fishermen who had found themselves in the wrong place at the wrong time. Only the wreckage of the boats remained, but the men were safe thanks to the help of the Nereids. Nereus's daughters often found themselves in similar events due to attacks by monstrous cousins, saving the lives of fishermen and sailors.

Nereus, from the Thapsos Peninsula, scanned the threatening sky and thought of his daughter Galateia bravely leaving on a mission. With a heavy heart, he prayed to the stars to guide her and to bring her back to him safe and sound.

That turmoil of the waters gave the sea a terrifying appearance; the leaden sky that announced a storm and the wind that started to blow violently created a creepy scenario.

From the lugubrious castle of Naxos, the black soldiers of King Adranos came galloping accompanied by a horde of Branchieres, those ravenous dogs, that bloodthirsty and terrifying molosser, ready to tear anyone to pieces.

What started from Naxos was the most horrendous army that had ever been seen, preceded by sea monsters that would have destroyed everything in their path: they had to hand over the entire island to their sovereign's hands and nothing could stop them.

Adranos looked up from the black tide of men and dogs that spread from his castle and toasted himself with a rich glass of black wine, produced in the countryside to the south by the inhabitants of Abola. He looked at his reflection in the golden cup and smiled contemptuously at his bloody will: the island would have been his. His greedy thoughts were interrupted by one who tortured him more: "Where is she? The young elf must be mine."

The king of the Sicels possessed five of the most ferocious dogs in the world, huge and muscular, they were his best servants, he only trusted them, and they were always by his side, their names were: Mors, Devil, Malus, War and Orto and obeyed like chosen soldiers.

"Go, my faithful companions, find the last-born elf and bring her to me soon. She will try to get back to the volcano, she must not arrive, EVER! Find her and kill anyone who accompanies her! Run, run as fast as you can."

The dogs excited by the words of their master left the castle running and barking scarily, while Adranos raised his chalice high, then greedily drank that black wine of the southern countryside.

It was raining heavily by now, the wind was very strong, and the lightning lashed the black sky, powerful thunder echoed on the island and shook those souls that had just started traveling, ready to do anything to save their world. It rained relentlessly on Tuia and Abeius and on Salix and his army of silver elves.

Chapter XVII

The general Salix of the hawthorn left towards the west was now far away when Tuia and Abeius left the eastern gates of the kingdom of Pantalica to go north, meeting the great volcano, the majestic Etna.

The rain made their figures confused but shone like lightning at every flash. Head down they went on side by side in silence, only the storm spoke. Tuia did not know that Abeius was listening to the earth and would pick up every little vibration so as not to be caught unprepared.

Lightning cut the sky in two. Abeius raised his head, opened his eyes wide and suddenly gave Tuia's horse a shot to make it start instantly, shouting: "Run, run as fast as you can!"

There was a frightening bark and two huge dogs threw themselves into the path, causing the horses to rear up. Tuia and Abeius were thrown to the ground, in the mud and one of the big dogs savagely assaulted the elf general.

Abeius took up his sword, but the damn dog leaped from side to side. He wounded it a couple of times on its paws, but the rain had made everything slippery and the elf struggled to stay in the attack position.

Suddenly, the beast struck him, knocking him to the ground, ready to devour him.

Tuia was stuck against a boulder by the other monstrous dog that growled menacingly at her. Perhaps because of fear or perhaps anger, Tuia's hair burned and she literally caught fire. From her hands left two fiery meteors that hit the dog in the chest, hurling it at the other who was fighting in the mud with Abeius.

Tuia fell to the ground, the general rushed to her: "Tuia! No!"

The young elf looked dead, her waxy face dirty with mud and her eyes closed. Abeius picked her up and began to climb quickly on a small hill.

The dogs got up and started chasing him, but the elf didn't stop, he had to put Tuia to safety, she had to survive, she couldn't succumb to her power, she had to live.

He found a hollow in the rock and left the unconscious elf there, drew his sword and turned to the horrible dogs that had arrived a few feet below him. "Gurth goth rim lye. Now you will die."

At his scream of elven war, the terrible barking of the molossers responded and threw himself on one of them with a drawn sword.

Astride the beast, he tried to hit the other dog that attacked him from every side, and it could not bite him because it could hurt its companion until it threw itself on Abeius who impaled it directly to the heart falling helpless on the mud.

The beast that the general rode, went mad with rage when it saw the other big dog on the ground dead and started violently to shake itself to make Abeius fall. Failing, it decided to turn around trying to crush the elf with its own weight. The sword escaped the general, he tried to keep those jaws far from his face with the strength of his hands.

One against the other, in the storm, in the slimy mud they fought to kill each other. Suddenly, the big dog opened its eyes and in slow motion, it fell dead on its side. Abeius lifted his head, as he removed the heavy beast from him, and saw her: Tuia stood on the hill with her bow in her hand and a half-smile on her face in that still pale face. She had shot her first arrow and killed a monstrous dog.

They looked at each other and exclaimed together:

"How are you?"

"Good."

"Damn it, what are these muscular monsters, dogs?"

Tuia had approached Abeius who was checking the big beasts turning them over to better observe them.

"These are the Branchieres, the molosser dogs of Adranos … He knows you are here, and he is hunting us."

Abeius looked at Tuia and already expected the fateful "why." He had to explain that even for a little while that man had been her father.

"Tuia in your past there was a brief period during which you had a family."

Abeius did not know how to continue, so, in the end, he merely set out the truth:

"You were the adopted daughter of King Adranos and Queen Thalia."

"What? I can't believe it … But what a loving father I had. And what were these creatures? Welcome back home gifts?"

Now she was really angry.

"I was born from a star and ended up in the hands of the most despicable man on the island … how to say, from the stars to the stables!"

"And yet, for what little you have been with them, they really loved you. The queen broke her heart when I took you away, it was she who decided that you should not run any danger and you had to disappear … She entrusted you to me." Abeius tried to explain to Tuia that her life in the arms of the royal family of Naxos had been brief but full of affection.

"Too bad the dear father was just thirsty for power, isn't that Abeius?"

"I think so … Even though he wanted to know you were safe … When I took you away, he seemed really sorry."

"It seemed!" Tuia pointed out with a hint of pungent irony. By now the young elf had learned to cushion emotional blows. Who knows how many things she had to discover about her elven past?

"By the way… and Queen Thalia? What do you tell me about my adoptive mother? Does she still live with that monstrous man?"

"Nobody has seen her since that night, the night of the battle against the Phoenicians. Among the Sicels, it is said that he killed her as a tribute to his immortality."

"Oh …" Tuia frowned and didn't know what to say. That last revelation struck her not a little.

Meanwhile, the rain was subsiding. The young elf had a pale face with tiredness and perhaps also with strong emotions created by the general's stories.

"Abeius I am tired and hungry; do we take advantage of that little cave on the hill you found to rest?"

Tuia was really white in the face. Abeius accompanied her to the shelter and went to look for something to eat. He didn't have to stray too far, because the area was rich in prickly pears and he already knew to give a nice surprise to the young elf who loved those sweet, pulpy fruits.

Tuia and Abeius ate greedily as a timid sun began peeping through the clouds. Etna was in front of them, grim, ready to be climbed, but every time the general looked up a shadow obscured his gaze.

Tuia slept a little while, Abeius remained on guard listening to the earth all the time.

The two elves resumed their journey through the Hyblaean Mountains and began a steep and slippery climb. On their right, on the coast, the Sicel villages, the Thapsos peninsula, and, on the Ionius Sea, the boats of fishermen who danced in the waves of the stormy sea ran. On the left, they left the Val of Netum, with its fields and vineyards to move ever further towards that territory dominated by the great volcano, changed over the centuries by the numerous eruptions that had made the surrounding area characterized by black lava stone.

Hidden the faces under the cloaks to prevent the travelers who met on the street from recognizing them, they climbed the mountains in silence, but Tuia's thoughts were abuzz with the latest revelations of Abeius: in a moment of despair, she thought that if she ever had had a family again.

The general was listening to every slightest sign, now that the rain was dying, he could more easily pick up every single vibration of the ground and from afar he heard loud noises: at the bottom of the valley, you could see the crossing of a black army of men and dogs.

"Tuia looks: the army of Adranos is already on the border of the kingdom of Pantalica … The elven defenses are impenetrable, they will never find the entrance, but they will seize Salix and his men behind while the sea monsters will attack them in front."

Abeius stopped for a moment and took a thin blade of grass from the ground and started blowing through it. An almost imperceptible hissing sounded out for about ten seconds, then the general waited.

"It is difficult to think of it, but I am sure that someone will hear me even with these clouds."

After about ten minutes, three peregrine falcons swooped down towards the elf general and landed on his muscular arms.

"Hawks! Oh, the wonder of nature, Abeius have they come for you?" Tuia was enchanted by so much beauty.

"I called them to bring my message to King Corylus, he must prepare his army for battle."

Abeius spoke and looked the falcon closer to its face. "She is Inessa, my best friend. She will carry the message, Katan and Mulciber will defend her in flight."

The other two hawks listened to the elf, proud of their mission. After having clearly understood what they had to do, the three hawks flew northwards towards the Green Valley of Alcantara to warn the wise king Corylus.

"Now let's try how much elven is awakened in you. Ready to run? We have at most ten hours to reach the volcano. An elf can run a lot without getting tired so now … run!"

Only a moment's hesitation and Tuia realized that Abeius was already speeding northward. She started running too: she had to keep up. In doing so they swallowed miles upon miles.

From afar a strong fog like a great wall seemed to want to block their way; a noise, a rush of water, and moist and warm air came towards them.

"Wait, that air is sulphurous. We have reached Lake Palikè, overcoming this, we will pass the plain of Katanè and begin the final ascent to the volcano."

Abeius scrutinized the strange mists and the surrounding areas rich in citrus orchards which, with their smell, contrasted those bad sulphur fumes.

"There is something strange in the middle of those mists … I see someone beckoning me to come closer. You wait here, I will go to the source and it won't bother me, I am made of fire."

Tuia turned to Abeius reassuring him, determined to go in the middle of that dense wall of steam. The general drew his sword and approached her at the fog bank but could not go further because those fumes were lethal to him. He watched the silhouette of the young elf approaching two others.

"The Palics … We have come to the lakes of Naftia, to their sacred lakes, where they bless the righteous and punish the liars," murmured Abeius to himself. He had recognized the outlines of the fortune tellers brothers, Guardians of the Air, and feared their revelations. How much could they have upset the young Tuia?

Meanwhile, Tuia had reached the muddy bank of the lake. Two figures dressed in white approached and as soon as they touched her shoulders, enormous geysers were released from two craters, like volcanic eruptions.

Tuia turned and saw two young boys, two twins with very green eyes that moved in symbiosis. They looked at her and smiled at her, then spoke to her with their mind; two voices as light as air, whose words seemed to fly like butterflies in that dense air.

"Tuia we are the Palics, Guardians of the Air. The exhalations of these waters are very important because they manage to unmask the perjurers. Approaching the waters, who swears before us is immediately punished if he is a false man. The jurors throw tablets into the water; that of those who said the truth will remain afloat, the other will sink and perjury will suffer the just punishment: blindness or death. We tell you this because you came here with an elf general and a Guardian of the Earth. He promised to protect you until his death, if his oath is valid, when you leave here you will find him unharmed, otherwise … Palikè spares no one be it man, elf or guardian."

"Abeius, no! Tuia screamed through the white wall of fog, but on the other side, nobody could hear anything, let alone Abeius.

"Listen to us, free your heart from bad thoughts, you are the star that will free the elven people from the curse, but you will save more than one race from extinction. Continue your journey, do not fear the dragon that has been waiting for you for centuries; the volcano is a kingdom to be discovered and liberated.

We give you three crystal ampoules; you will need them to collect the firewater with which you will cure souls and wounds caused by the poisonous claws of those evil sea monsters. Don't beat yourself up, an old sage will tell you what to do; have no prejudice against anyone; go ahead with instinct and loyalty and then the way will be clear to you. We say goodbye to you, sister."

The two young men kissed Tuia on the forehead and disappeared into one of the sulfur craters. Gradually the dense wall of fog disappeared, revealing an Abeius with a drawn sword, ready to face any enemy. Tuia ran to him and hugged him as if she hadn't seen him for centuries, leaving him surprised. "Abeius dear, I'm so happy to see you!"

And kissed him on the cheeks so many times that the general blushed violently.

"I am happy that you are finally out of all that fog. They were the Palics, right?"

Abeius broke away from Tuia and tried to compose himself, but he really liked that gesture of affection from the young girl.

"Yes, it was the Palics … Look what I have here. Tuia showed him the three crystal ampoules.

"I understood. It really is an important thing. Come on, let's continue the climb, now that the fog is dissolved. We will pass the plain of Katanè quickly and soon we will climb on the black rocks of the southern slope of your volcano."

The two elves ran, and the Sicel villages were left behind, the Etna valley flowed beneath their feet and began to be colored with black lava stone where chestnut, hazelnut, cherry, and fragrant apple trees grew.

A breathtaking landscape appeared whenever they stopped to contemplate the territory beneath them: it was the scenery that reflected the infinite sea, the magnificent coasts and the lush green of their enchanting and wild island. That was the moment when their hearts filled with courage and they left again: their beloved Trinacria had to be saved.

The elves ran and climbed like panthers, fast against the wind and against the rain that had begun to fall again insistently.

The plain of Katanè was now behind them, it seemed that there was not so much the fog was thick, but the elves, even though the thickest haze, had glimpsed the Adranos' branchieres: three large dogs were at their heels determined to interrupt their journey to the crater central of the volcano, where the great dragon Typhoeus resided, and to capture the young elf to bring to their greedy King.

Abeius had already heard the movements of the enormous and bloodthirsty beasts for a while and he was determined to get more advantage, even if Tuia would have gladly stopped among those majestic chestnuts, to smell the air that smelled of apples.

Suddenly something attracted their attention: overhanging you could see the city of Naxos in the valley inhabited by the Sicels, on Mount Tauro there was a black castle, the fortress of King Adranos, from where you could notice a black river of men went out and marched south.

Among the heavy clouds of rain came a ray of sunshine and Tuia was fascinated by a shy rainbow: she had always dreamed of being able to get on that colored bridge. Although annoyed by the stop of the young elf, Abeius was struck by that fantastic panorama made of black clouds and color, a bridge of hope.

But that distraction cost them a lot: the evil dogs were very close and by now they were almost on them. Abeius drew his sword and before the three ravenous molossers came out of the bushes Tuia shot her second lethal arrow; the big dog that suddenly jumped over the brambles, fell rolling on the mud struck in the chest.

The second Branchiere dog, sheltered behind the first, had deflected another arrow from Tuia, but Abeius struck it with his powerful sword, cutting off its paw. The third collided with the general elf and jumped from side to side trying to dodge the blows inflicted by Abeius. This time Tuia, climbed a boulder, got the bow focused on the enemy to hit. The tip of the arrow caught fire and resolutely hurled it at the mutilated Branchiere, killing it.

Abeius had already wounded the big beast that was struggling with him, it was dying and staggering, but when he came to deliver the fatal blow, he came into contact with the animal that was on the ground in agony: "What is your name?"

"I am Mors, elf and I am dying … Freeing myself from this horrible gall that I carry on myself, all his pain turned into hate."

"Who are you talking about? Reply…"

Abeius tried to shake the huge beast, but it didn't speak anymore. "What do you have Abeius? You look upset." Tuia had approached the body of the big dog checking if it was still alive and had noticed that the elf stared at it in shock.

"I managed to get in touch with its mind … A poor soul poisoned by its master's hatred," said Abeius, looking at Tuia as if to focus on her face.

"It spoke of great pain and me… I heard him." Tuia looked at Abeius but did not understand what he meant by those words; they walked slowly away from the bodies of large dogs, in silence as if out of respect for those dead.

"Now it's just the two of us: Adranos' faithful stalwarts are dead and you are almost there. Turn around, lookup and you'll see the central crater: the great hole is the cave of Typhoeus, the dragon of the volcano."

Abeius indicated the summit of Etna, with great respect for such great grandeur and majesty, "A Muntagna" ruled above them.

With eyes turned upward, Tuia could see smoke and a large hole surrounded by black lava stone. She had arrived, but she still had something to do.

She began to strip off the precious armor she was wearing, she could not have taken it with her, the heat of the volcano would have ruined it.

"Abeius, you will bury it here, so when the princess of the hawthorn comes out of the volcano, she can finally wear it."

The young Greener handed over the silver armor but kept the sword with her: "I don't have a sword of mine, did you notice Abeius? I'll take this with me … You never know that the dragon will want to eat me, and I will have to defend myself," said Tuia, looking at Abeius, with a mischievous smile.

He calmly answered her: "If you had ever had such a doubt, you would never have gone alone into the volcano, little Greener. However, you can keep it, you can deliver it yourself to King Anax's daughter when you're in there."

Tuia and Abeius looked at each other smiling and hid the precious armor underground, then Tuia took Abeius's hands:

"My dear friend, I'm going, don't worry about me, we'll meet soon."

She greeted him with a kiss on the cheek but could not look him in the eye.

Abeius followed her with his eyes until he saw her disappear inside the volcano: the little fiery star had really returned home.

Then he picked a blade of grass from the ground and as he did when he was with Tuia he blew through it. He didn't have to wait long for his trusted partner. Mulciber landed on his powerful arm: "I'm glad you're healthy and safe Mulciber. You will stay here and when Tuia leaves the volcano you will come to tell me."

"And now it's my turn … King Corylus and his hawks await me."

He took a last look at the smoky cave where Tuia had entered and then the falcon general set off quickly towards the Green Valley of Alcantara.

Two watchful eyes remained to contemplate the almost bare area on a high branch of a chestnut tree: those of Mulciber the faithful peregrine falcon proud of its mission.

Chapter XVIII

Beyond the Hymera River, in the western part of the island, in Motyon, the elves of the hawthorn had found a Sican settlement, a stronghold where there was a simple village made of huts and a rustic fence of boulders and logs tree, nothing so strong that it can withstand an external attack.

The Elymians and Sicans, allies for some time, were determined to fight to defend their territory. At the arrival of the elven army, they exulted with hope and opened the gates to let their salvation enter.

Salix was received by the generals of the two peoples: the general of the Elymians was called Mozio and Inico the one of the Sicans, two muscular men, could be seen from their arms that had fought numerous battles hard, their scars told their arduous struggles. They welcomed Salix as an old friend and were especially pleased to see that their elf neighbors had provided them with food, fruit, vegetables, and numerous baskets of bread.

They talked to the general of the hawthorn for a long time, showing on the maps how they had taken care to protect their borders. They had even raised a new and majestic wall within their territories to protect the city of Krastos where they had left women and children and where the king resided with his bride, whose marriage had united the two kingdoms as the queen was the daughter of the deceased king of Elymians.

General Mozio was a very good strategist and his plan to make the city impregnable was pleasing to Salix, but the man never expected to hear what the elf would reveal to him.

"Valiant companions, I admire your great dowry in organizing your villages and the fact that you have worked so hard at the inner stronghold of Krastos leaves me quite impressed. Fortified your inner-city where leaving women and children is a point in our favor but I would dare to say that here in Motyon we can not hope to do it, neither with the monsters nor with the black army of Adranos ..."

Salix could not finish his speech when the two strong men jumped like springs.

"Monsters? We have not seen monsters ..." Mozio beat his fists on the sturdy table where there was the map with the attack strategies, surely, he had been shocked by the revelation of Salix.

"Let me talk, you didn't know anything because none of your men came back alive from an encounter with those evil beasts."

"Exactly, elf, they are Ceto and Phorcys, Echidna and Ladon, and to the north-eastern coast Scylla and Charybdis, unfortunately, they belong to my family but surely my father Nereus will fight them with you by sea because he is a wise man and a guardian of water."

A girl, strong and daring, entered the tent of the generals and surprised them by interfering in the already heated discussion, behind her came running a boy made of grass and leaves.

"Salix how nice to see you again!" Rosewood had jumped on his hawthorn's general, very happy to meet again a friendly face.

"Well, who do we have here? The little leaf elf we had lost and a damsel coming from the sea. As far as my eyes can see you have seen bad moments. Why?"

Salix shifted his questioning gaze from Rosewood to the young woman.

"My name is Galateia and I am a nereid, one of the fifty daughters of Nereus. I have a mission to do: I must go to Selinos by the Gorgons to deliver a precious item that they will keep until the rightful owner claims it.

On the way, I was attacked by Ladon, as were the men who were there to protect your borders. No one survived and even I would have died if it hadn't been for this leaf elf that fought valiantly. Then the monster vanished into the woods."

"And so, I decided to go with her," Rosewood finished proud of himself.

"Obviously" Salix reiterated, knowing the meddling character of the leaf elf, as he tried to apologize to the other two generals, who were left open-mouthed listening to all that sudden confusion. "Mozio, Inico humbly ask you to welcome and refresh these two friends of mine, miraculously alive and bearers of news."

The general of the hawthorn was very worried, he had Rosewood and Galateia taken to a small hut where they would rest, while he and the other two generals discussed all night how the walls should be reinforced and how they should handle the attack.

Already from the first light of dawn men and elves worked tirelessly at the fortification of the walls, at the creation of new weapons, some secretly admired the glittering silver elven armor with their precious weapons.

Salix gave the two generals two indestructible elf swords, blessed at dawn by the new sun, as a sign of an alliance between elves and men. Then he went to the hut where Rosewood and Galateia had been received.

He found Galateia ready for departure and Rosewood arguing with her because he was still determined to accompany her; she seemed adamant.

"Good morning, ready to go? You can be escorted by some soldiers up to the walls of Krastos, from the inside of the city you can head south-west towards Selinos. I listened to your attack on Pantalica, a poor wretch had managed to save himself and reach our borders; he spoke of strange movements of tree roots. Rosewood, it was you, wasn't it? You've been good. What is your mission Nereus's daughter?"

Salix was anxious to understand what a dangerous mission could push her out of the sea.

"We can't know," Rosewood answered sarcastically.

"I need to understand why you risk your life. The armies of Adranos are close and if they can be stopped, I can't say the same of your monstrous cousins."

"I can't reveal anything … I promised my father and I would be grateful if you didn't insist on asking me anymore." Determined Galateia looked into the elven general's eyes as a sign of challenge.

They came out of the hut and were surrounded by a black cloud, by a rustling like wings and leaves stirred by the wind from which Gabrys, the bat, materialized.

“Rosewood, little prickly pear thorn, I finally found you alive and well. I’m relieved.”

Gabrys squeezed the little leaf elf with a hug and then turned to his general friend: “Salix, the monster Ladon is hidden a few miles from the Hymera river. Perhaps it awaits the arrival of the black army or, worse still, the ravenous Adranos’ branchieres. Get ready, I will go to warn King Anax so he will leave immediately for the battle.”

“Galateia, if you’re still determined to leave, go now or you won’t have time left. You will have to be fast. Rosewood if these walls fall, we will come back on Krastos.”

Rosewood listened to Salix, stiff and resolute, the general of the hawthorn had awakened in him that sense of courage and honor that he had often kept for himself, avoiding getting into trouble.

“Very good general, we will arrive in Krastos before sunset. Within the walls, we will be safer and by tomorrow, Galateia will be at Selinos. Let the stars guide us.”

Gabrys hugged him and put a small black fife in his hand.

“This is the black pipino, it serves to call me.”

The witch and the little leaf elf looked at each other in silence, then Rosewood took Galateia by the hand and began to run.

The young nereid managed only to look up and meet Salix’s blue eyes, then walked away pulled by the leaf elf, determined to quickly abandon what would soon be a dangerous battlefield.

“May the stars protect you.”

Gabrys and Salix prayed at the same time while with their eyes they accompanied the two now distant figures of Rosewood and Galateia that disappeared amid high poplars.

Suddenly a horn was heard in the distance and Salix paled: that sound warned of immediate danger, he turned and saw a soldier approach running.

"An army of men in black is approaching with a horde of Adranos hideous dogs, general!"

Salix was already thinking about how to move and he had started giving definite orders to everyone, elves, and men. "Climb up the walls and prepare the bows! Dogs must not go beyond the walls! I fear them more than black soldiers, they are lethal, ravenous beasts and devour their enemies. No, they must not reach anyone, be it a man or an elf!" Salix climbed the ramparts to scan the forest in front, he already saw and felt the approach of the enemy army.

Sicans and Elimyans ran to the walls armed to the teeth, side by side like brothers to fight for their lives, for their families, and their land. The arrival of the elves had brought them some hope but, in their eyes, one could read the terror: they knew that those dogs were evil and poisonous beasts and at the thought of it the blood in the veins was frozen.

The magnificent and lethal hawthorn's elves waited with their bows on the stronghold's walls ready to shoot their arrows at the signal of their beloved general, waiting for the right moment next to his bat witch friend.

"Are we ready, general?"

"Always."

Salix raised his right arm and shouted: "Gurth goth rim lye, To death our enemies!"

Gabrys turned into a giant black bat and flew toward the kingdom of Pantalica. The great war had begun: the elven, shining and deadly arrows were hurled toward the forest where a black army emerged like the dangerous waves of a stormy sea, big dogs accompanied the soldiers, but fell mowed under the elven darts.

Salix had given orders that part of his army leave for the city of Krastos to guard the walls: he had a bad feeling, if Abeius had not arrived on time he could already count on his men on the spot.

With this idea on his head, he raised his eyes to the sky looking for the protection of the stars. The day had risen, it was not raining, and the air was sultry due to the evaporation of the rain of the day before. It was a hot day in all senses and the battle would be fiery.

The enemies fell under the arrows of the elves, the walls held up and the generals shouted their orders so that all the corners of the fortification were covered: they could not allow the enemies to weaken them.

The black soldiers never ended, at least ten others came from a fallen man and by now they were already dangerously close to the walls, they came out of the thick trees of the forest with very strong ladders for the siege of the ramparts.

With a chilling scream, Ladon, a monstrous marine beast, showed himself, pulling behind him an enormous catapult that he loaded with huge boulders.

The men of Adranos began to climb over the walls and the defenses began to give way even though Elymians and Sicans proved to be skilled in combat: the black army was endless and invincible with that monster as an ally.

The hours passed and already in the early afternoon men and elves began to despair, Ladon had almost knocked down the fortification by throwing boulders and many black soldiers were already inside the city.

Salix looked at the sky. A black cloud was approaching, and the elf heaved a sigh of relief: they were Gabrys's bats, which meant that the reinforcements were now close, hope returned.

Gabrys materialized next to General Salix and his command thousands of black bats attacked the enemy soldiers giving a little respite to elves, Elymians and Sicans, who remained confused by that attack from above. The monster went mad, wriggled as if trying to chase away flies; the army of Adranos fought against those wild, unpredictable and winged creatures, which bitterly bit them with their sharp teeth.

"Gabrys arrived on time, the defenses were failing." Salix turned thankful to his witch friend.

"A great diversion waiting for King Anax and his troops to arrive and suddenly catch them."

Gabrys was satisfied with her timeliness.

Salix, however, thought of Rosewood and Galateia, which should have already crossed the walls of Krastos and headed for Selinos.

In reality, escorted by some soldiers, the young leaf elf and the nereid had come to the inside of the fortified city, but Galateia had decided to continue to Selinos alone, explaining to Rosewood that for him approaching the temple of the Gorgons could prove fatal. Rosewood had to give in and let go of Galateia because he had the order given by Salix, as spokesman for the elves, to go to the royal palace of Krastos to warn the king and the queen of danger and the possibility of taking refuge in the Old Mountain, in the Sicans Mountains, with women, old people and children, leaving the city isolated.

Galateia left on the back of a horse, galloping in the afternoon to arrive in Selinos.

Heading towards the royal palace of Krastos, Rosewood observed the apparent calm of the town. Children, the elderly and women filled the streets, you could see in the eyes of women the fear, the alertness, but also the strength of the protection of mothers.

The elders entertained the children by telling them ancient legends and stories of battles of the Trinacria, their beloved island.

The young leaf elf was afraid for those people; he had already seen the horrors that those monsters could create and was determined to protect the city first-hand. His place would have been on the ramparts, the trees would have helped him, whatever the danger would have been. Rosewood tried to encourage himself, until his friend Gabrys surfaced in his mind, reassuring him that her little pipino tied to his neck gave him courage.

The bat and the king's soldiers would have arrived as soon as possible, then he thought of Tuia … where was Tuia?

Chapter XIX

Tuia had finished her climb and now stared at the entrance to a cave, the dragon's cave. In the last twenty-four hours, she had traveled many kilometers, killed monstrous dogs, discovered she had a family and that the dear father longed for her death; what was waiting for her now?

The young Greener thought of all this by looking at what appeared in front of her: strange darkness, a fluctuating black, as if to close that warm cavern there was a sheet of black velvet that sinuously moved in the warm breath that came from inside.

A moment's hesitation and then the awareness that it was what she had to do, so she took a step and let herself be enveloped by the darkness.

She felt strangely wet as if bathed in hot steam, and when she opened her eyes, she found herself inside a sparkling cave, where the walls reflected the fire that appeared before her.

That fire stirred, became animated and took life in a hundred little flames: little men made of the fire looked at her as if in adoration and one of them came forward with a cloak of black velvet. It seemed to be made of the same substance that closed the entrance to the cave and it was at that point that Tuia realized she was completely naked: her light little dress, at that heat, had practically evaporated. She did not hesitate for a moment to wear what the little man gave her.

Suddenly the flames knelt and shouted: "Long live the queen."

"No, no, no, Queen?" I think you're a little confused."

While Tuia tried to understand that situation, a small flame beckoned to her to follow him, the others opened the road and pushed her to go down steep stairs carved into the rock.

The young elf was curious but also intimidated by what she would find at the bottom of the stairs; the red light was more intense and when she reached the last step she looked out to see what was beyond: the flames, then, lifted her weight and carried her inside a huge cave, it was the dragon's cave.

Tuia literally froze at the sight of the enormous beast: as it was impossible to freeze inside a volcano, she shivered from head to toe.

A majestic, magnificent specimen of a dragon with gold scales, slept in the center of the enormous cavern. "Wonderfully scary," she thought.

She could not speak and there was no need because someone was already waiting for her.

"You finally arrived, my daughter, he waited for you so long … First, he damned himself, then he became sad and cried so much that he lost all his strength, so much that he no longer had the desire to continue to live. You were his jewel as you were for me … I repaid my debt by offering my life as a gift, forever, to the great and powerful Etna and now you are back … and you are the queen."

"Who are you? Tuia asked that woman, but perhaps she had already understood.

"I am Queen Thalia, your mother, little star of the firmament. Allow me to embrace you … my soul has burned for centuries inside the Etna and now you come as a cool stream. The stars have listened to my tears once more, and had compassion on a mother's suffering."

She ran towards the young elf and embraced her crying, kissed her face, her hands; happiness had finally come to her.

Tuia didn't know whether to feel happy, but surely, she was very very confused, she had to collect the pieces of the puzzle of that life that was slowly reforming. She could not speak and succumbed to the embraces of the unknown "mother."

Suddenly some little flames took Queen Thalia and forcibly displaced her, the woman fell to the side, smiling and crying overwhelmed by that surprise, but she knew that Tuia had something important to do: she had to wake the dragon.

The flames circled around the young elf and the sleeping Typhoeus, but Tuia didn't know what to do. She instinctively approached and with her left hand, pushed by a strange sensation, touched the scaly brow of the dragon.

A sharp pain ripped through her chest and Tuia's screams echoed throughout the cave. The flames began to twirl like crazy, the fire exploded: Etna had returned to rumble on the island and Typhoeus had reopened his large serpentine eyes.

Tuia was on the ground, the strong pain had dazed her and made her fall. She looked at the burning imprint on her chest before raising her eyes and seeing her face reflected in the green eyes of the majestic dragon.

She felt his pain, the pain experienced by that huge beast and then she saw tears, big hot tears coming down from Typhoeus's luminous eyes. He wept as Queen Thalia had done and she felt the emotion go up to her throat, a knot that melted and freed her from pain and fear.

Some little flames took turns under the great dragon, they had with them the ampoules that the Palics had given to Tuia and gathered the big tears, Tuia looked into Typhoeus's eyes and saw the love he felt for her, so she stroked him on the huge head consoling his pain until the dragon calmed down.

Suddenly, a deep voice, which Tuia did not understand where it came from, spoke to her: "You have finally returned to me, little star of fire. You are the queen of Etna, you who hold the fate of the island. I have hurt your people by mistakenly destroying a magical artefact called Triskelion, condemning the elves to sterility, but you are the last-born elf and you will give them their life back. I made mistakes in my past and now I am ready to make up for it, fighting with you and for you. When you're ready, we'll leave and fight together."

Typhoeus spoke with Tuia with his mind and she magically felt and could answer him.

"I am honored to be here with you. I love my Island and I love this volcano, whose fire flows inside me as a Greener, I will defend it with my life itself."

"I will defend your life," said Typhoeus proudly.

"Then you'll have to do it with Abeius," Tuia replied ironically.

"Abeius? Why is that elf here? I don't even want to see him; I could kill him."

The Dragon stirred frighteningly, causing Tuia to fall to the ground, awed by the sudden jerk.

"But he saved my life and protected me, he brought me here to you!" shouted the young elf with all the breath she had in her body and almost ready to burst into tears.

"If he hadn't taken you I would have taken care of you," Typhoeus replied, who brought his big head close to Tuia, tiny against that huge dragon, and looked into her eyes.

The young elf gathered all her courage and shouted to him: "That was my destiny, our destiny! Now I'm here thanks to him and I think you should be grateful to him."

The enormous dragon sagged and in a calm and gentle voice replied: "Yes, I am grateful to him, but I envy the time he spent with you."

Tuia got up from the ground and went to embrace the big head of Typhoeus, a single tear came down from the dragon's big eyes and Tuia picked it up with her hands. A little flame came up with an ampoule, looking happily at its Queen, and picked up the last tear of fire: the dragon Typhoeus would no longer cry.

A woman remained in a corner in silence. Tuia had almost forgotten her, it was Typhoeus who beckoned her to come closer, so she did and silently embraced her.

"Why are you here. queen Thalia?"

Tuia did not dare call her mum or mother, she had a human mother and did not know how to behave.

"When Abeius took you away through the portal of time, your father, King Adranos, betrayed the pact of an alliance between elves and men, allying with monsters. I don't know the reason for his gesture, or what demon he might have recommended but he bartered my life for his immortality. I am alive thanks to the elven queen Silene who came to tell me what my husband was about to do. She wanted to take me to the Green Kingdom of Alcantara, but I had already done too much damage to the elven people. Desperate, I decided to offer my life to the dragon instead because in that whole story I was the only one to die."

"But you are alive, after all these centuries. How?" Tuia was now curious to know all the events.

"Typhoeus is not a bloodthirsty beast: he took pity on my suffering. He didn't kill me but in exchange, I had to offer my children to the volcano."

Tuia listened with an open mouth.

"This fire is magical … From my sterile belly two twins were born, two Greeners that I think you have already met. They have no name, they only call them Palics because they often meet among the sulphur sources of Palikè."

Queen Thalia turned to the flames, staring at the phials that Tuia had received in Palike' from the two strangest men she had ever seen.

"That's why they called me sister." Tuia paused to think of the twins.

"And the dragon didn't even kill the three of us."

Three female elves sprang from behind Typhoeus and ran to meet Tuia, very surprised.

"I've already heard of you! You are the daughters of King Anax of the kingdom of Pantalica and you, you are his queen."

Tuia was starting to smile, she was really happy to see all those people alive and well.

"So Typhoeus … Blessed among women, eh?"

Tuia laughed and looked at her magnificent dragon, stood up to contemplate the cave, and then suddenly asked a question Typhoeus: "Typhoeus but female dragons do not exist? I can't believe you're the only one left."

"I was waiting for you to find my race. This island has undergone conquests and looting by numerous invaders over the centuries, many dragons have been killed and others have moved to other islands. I stood defending the Trinacria and my volcano … And blinded by anger I made the mistake of attacking the elves from the northern islands, destroying their future, the Triskelion."

"Then we will leave as soon as possible, we will visit the other dragons and they will help us defeat the sea monsters and save the island!"

Tuia was excited now.

"But where?" Typhoeus was skeptical.

"We will fly north to the islands of volcanoes."

Tuia was firm and confident about where their adventure would take them. Not being able to hear the discussion between the minds of the young elf and the majestic dragon, the four women looked on curiously, until Tuia turned to speak to them:

"We will leave Etna soon. You will return to Pantalica to king Anax, Abeius will come to pick you up."

She paused a moment, looked at Queen Thalia and said, "Mother… mother you too will go to Pantalica, it will be safer."

"Light of my eyes, I will remain here waiting for your return. I belong to the volcano there is no safer place for me."

Tuia looked at her. She could not tell her anything, that she was sorry for what had happened to her and that she wanted to explain to her that it was too early to really consider her mother.

Queen Thalia approached, stroked her face and as if she had listened to Tuia's thoughts, she said to her: "Don't worry about me, my daughter, you have nothing to say, reassure your storm soul because you have returned home."

Then the four women looked at each other smiling and ran to get something.

The youngest of King Anax's two daughters, Daisy, excitedly explained to Tuia and Typhoeus what was happening:

"Well dear Tuia, we knew you would come back. We have waited so long, but we have also worked a lot, creating for you a splendid armor, with the precious metal of the volcano, worked with flames and decorated by the lovely hands of your mother. My sister and my mother, on the other hand, have worked on a battle saddle for dragons woven by the skillful hands of an elf queen and an armor for Typhoeus, obviously aided by the tireless flame men, as was done in the ancient lands for the dragon knights, so that they can serve you in the battle that will free our island from the evil monsters and the elven population from the curse."

That said, the four women knelt and placed the precious gifts at the feet of Tuia and Typhoeus.

"Wow …" the elf and the dragon exclaimed together, pleasantly surprised.

Tuia was entranced by the splendor of those precious gifts forged for her when something occurred to her: "Oh, I have something that belongs to you, princess …"

From a sheath tied to her waist, she pulled out an elegant silver-plated elven sword with the hawthorn's crest.

"Oh, this is mine! My father had it made for my feast of maturity with a wonderful armor."

The princess's face darkened for a moment but then she smiled and introduced herself:

"Well, I am Robinia, the firstborn of King Anax of the Kingdom of Pantalica, she is my sister Daisy and my mother, Queen Vitalba."

"Nice to meet you, I'm Tuia, I'm a Greener of fire and last-born elf."

Tuia joked a little about her condition, even though she wanted to be someone else, thinking about what she still had to face.

It was time to leave, Tuia wore a sparkling golden armor, reinforced by volcanic metal, embellished with rubies and emeralds extracted from her beloved Etna. Typhoeus also had complete armor for dragons, a helmet of black metal set with precious stones, and forearms of the same alloy combined with equally engraving, which made him magnificent and terrible, the wonderful black leather saddle had been tied to his back, adorned with sparkling gems and gold.

Tuia stood looking at her dragon for a long time, his magnificence was worthy of being praised forever. If she had thought of it well Typhoeus was already a legendary dragon, but for her, at that time it represented just the power and majesty of a volcano, he was the Etna.

And now they were in front of the great opening of the cave, one next to the other, and together they would open the passage closed by the spell. Tuia beckoned to Typhoeus, then with her face turned to the floating black that closed the entrance, she concentrated, brought her hands forward and shouted some magic words suggested by the dragon: "Focus Impera!"

At those words uttered together, Typhoeus spat fire and Tuia exploded two fiery meteors that struck the spell, and the black velvet dissipated like vapor in the cool evening air.

As soon as she left the volcano, Tuia looked towards the place where she had left Abeius and was invaded by enormous happiness because her general was there waiting for her with Mulciber on one arm and a delegation of elves, the falcons of King Corylus of the Green Valley of the Alcantara.

Chapter XX

The volcano was active again, it had awakened after so long and now it roared in all its power. The lava flowed out quickly and glowed down the eastern slope; the sky was burning with lapilli and Tuia and the huge dragon Typhoeus were ready to leave. The young elf came down from Abeius carrying the four women with her.

Abeius was surprised and delighted to see Queen Thalia again. "Regina Thalia, my friend, how can you be here … yet?"

Abeius could not understand, but Tuia beckoned to him that, at another time, she would explain it, now he had to bring the elves to Pantalica.

"They are the princesses of the kingdom of Pantalica, Robinia and Daisy and this is Queen Vitalba, wife of King Anax. Escort them to Pantalica; I have to leave with Typhoeus. We'll be back soon, let's go hunting for dragons."

Tuia would not have wanted to leave his friend Abeius so soon but had to find the dragons as she had promised Typhoeus.

"Dragons?"Abeius was baffled.

"Even Typhoeus has a right to a future: it has been too long for him alone and then, if I can bring some here, they can help us against sea monsters. I have to put the Triskelion back together, so those treacherous creatures will die. Salix needs you, go Abeius that the stars protect you."

Tuia was unrecognizable: the child no longer existed; she was now a true warrior. Not to mention her appearance, the armor that had created the elves for her inside the volcano gave her an air of power.

The long red hair had been combed by the delicate hands of Queen Thalia in two long braids and on the head shone a kind of gilded helmet wherein the center the Triskelion had been engraved, a symbol that excelled also on the armor bodice.

Abeius had been struck by the sight of so much beauty, Tuia had in herself the power and magnificence of Etna and reflected the character of the volcano that she had awakened.

Queen Thalia greeted her general friend and then kissed Tuia in the forehead, without saying a word, without a tear. She trusted Typhoeus, she knew he would protect her and bring her back safe and sound. Elegant and silent, she returned to the volcano.

Abeius put the three elves on horses and gave orders to his soldiers to escort them to Pantalica. He would go to meet King Corylus, who was already heading west towards the Sican territory.

He could not take his eyes off Tuia then, perhaps to distract himself from her, he turned to look at the erupting volcano:

“She finally woke up, the “Muntagna.” The Sicel people call it so reverently. Since the volcano no longer erupted, the island had lost its power. Typhoeus is the power and you represent her, you Tuia, you are the queen.”

Tuia blushed smugly but it was getting late and she had to reluctantly leave Abeius: first she would leave, first, she would return.

“My little warrior, I have something for you here. This is Etnah the black sword of the volcano, forged by the blind druid Silva of Green Valley of the Alcantara, using the black meteor that brought you here hundreds of years ago. Now it’s yours, Queen of the volcano.”

Abeius, solemnly, offered the black shining sword to Tuia, who knelt honored by that gift: she was moved and speechless. Then she said seriously and decisively: “I have to go, he is waiting for me. I will be back soon, and we will save our world.”

She embraced her general and felt great emotion, she recognized the smell of her beloved fir and felt something strange inside her, like a different heat. She stood aside and looked at Abeius in his wonderful green eyes; she had never noticed the depth of that look. She hugged him again and then with downcast eyes said: “See you soon.”

It was the second time she had moved away from him, but Abeius felt it was dangerous this time. It seemed that the soul broke in half, but it was just so: she had become a warrior, all her elven nature had by now blossomed; looking at her filled him with pride even though he knew she could now do without him. But he had promised about his life that he would protect her at all costs, and it would have been, forever.

Tuia climbed up to the entrance of the cave from where Typhoeus came out ready to face the skies, climbed on him, tied the straps tight, put on the golden boots in the stirrups, clung tightly to the spines and then whispered: "I am ready."

Typhoeus spat fire and roared with all his might, then threw himself off the cliff into the valley. Tuia screamed for the terrible feeling of emptiness never experienced in her life, that was freedom, the terror of flying and then liberation in a scream, feeling the soul go away and then come back, like dying and reliving, like lightning and the thunder, just like that the elf and her dragon felt.

The dragon increased his speed dramatically until he veered north and then rose again, slamming his magnificent golden wings that shone on the sunset, reflecting the redness of the lava that had begun to descend towards the east coast.

Abeius followed the departure of Tuia and Typhoeus until they disappeared on the horizon. He looked at the sky and saw the Perseids shine in the clear sky, then he realized that his precious elf had nothing to fear.

"Ireland will be our next destination. Fly Typhoeus, as fast as you can."

"I have no idea what this Ireland is and where it is," the doubtful dragon replied.

"Trust me, my friend," said Tuia, smiling.

The young elf felt the strong excitement of her dragon: he had finally returned to roaring, spitting fire and flying; his mood was like Etna's fire, a volcanic eruption not seen for centuries. Now he had his flame, she who had rekindled his life, and led him to new discoveries, now no one could touch her or even get close without his consent. She was his queen, only his pure soul could have woken him up and given him back the infinite sky.

Typhoeus was grateful for the precious gift.

Tuia welcomed within herself every little emotion of her dragon, now she flew through the clouds, into the vastness of the sky in which she had always fantasized, she felt the air in her face and wanted to touch the stars. In the infinite sea below them appeared small dots, islands and archipelagos.

Looking at her sea, she was moved, the tears started to fall on her face and joined the deep abyss to be part of it forever.

On earth, it was already dark, but she enjoyed the light of the firmament, of those protective stars that shone for her that night. The constellation of the Dragon and the Perseids seemed as fiery as the Etna left behind them, which erupted in all its power.

Tuia thought that her dream as a child had become reality, but suddenly she remembered: "The child!"

A shadow obscured her happiness. She had forgotten who she was: she hadn't thought for a while about that little girl in danger and the family that was suffering. Typhoeus warned that moment of bewilderment of his precious elf and asked her: "Little flame, what saddens you?"

Then Tuia told her dragon all that had happened to her since she arrived in Trinacria through the temporal limbo.

Typhoeus had no doubts: "Where you will go, I will go my queen, always with you."

Enormously grateful to the words of her dragon friend, Tuia felt encouraged and tried to concentrate positively on her mission.

"Thank you, my precious friend. We will find the dragons; we will attack the black army of Adranos and save the elves and … the little Tuia."

Tuia clung to the spines of Typhoeus while the dragon veered to better exploit the air currents that blew from the north and continued to reflect on all that she had lived. She thought of Salix and Abeius: she was confused about the feelings that bound her to both, then she tried to leave that thought behind and tried to concentrate on the flight trying to connect to Typhoeus as much as possible to share the wonders she saw through the sensations and the visions he transmitted to her.

And then it occurred to her, a story that she loved as a child: a lucky dragon and a boy who would save the world, a kind of hero … Although, in reality, in her story, the heroine had to be her. In the absurdity of the story of her life, all this was real, and she was living it: brought back in time by a strange force, the Magic of Nature, as her elf general had revealed to her.

Etna was in full swing and at the black castle, on one of its tall towers, King Adranos screamed like a madman. He was angry, a savage rage had seized him when he had seen the erupting volcano and seen the dragon and his fire, which, like a golden flash, tore through the sky.

"Bloody Hell! The elf has come to the volcano, and the dragon is awake! Incompetent! Where are those monsters? My faithful dogs had to stop her, but she has now joined the beast!"

His subordinates were all with their faces on the ground to put up with the wrath of their black king, petrified by terror. The columns and walls of those black rooms rumbled with screams as King Adranos growled like a mad dog.

"Prepare my horse, all ready to go with me! Even Ceto and Phorcys will march against those damn elves!"

Then he paused to think, "They're flying north, what does it mean? Why? This, however, will give us more time to go into battle and permanently eliminate the elven race from my island."

Adranos ruminated to himself, trampling his servants. He was blinded by anger and furiously armed himself to go to war.

The umpteenth horde of black soldiers came out of the castle of Naxos, this time headed by their king and headed for the coast where Ceto and Phorcys were already waiting for them.

Would they dare to tell King Adranos that Tuia's green sphere of thoughts had been stolen? So thought the sea monsters as they watched the army of the Sicels king approaching.

"Adranos we are ready, the elves will rot under our feet."

Ceto welcomed the allied king with a chilling war cry, Phorcys dared not say anything thinking of the trouble he had combined.

"Today the kingdom of the elves will fall, and I will command the whole Trinacria! We have to do it soon before the dragon comes back."

Silence and then a terrifying scream: "TO WAR!" The army set off at a gallop. The sea monsters would attack from the coast, going up the Kalikos river.

Nereus and his daughters had witnessed the departure of that cursed army from behind a cliff, they could not remain to do nothing, he had to join the elves: "We are not strong, but we can manage the sea. Dear daughters, we cannot fight on land, but the inhabitants of the abyss can help us. Together with sharks, dolphins and killer whales we can hinder and oppose my notorious brothers."

The forty-nine Nereids set out to "recruit" all the marine beings they could trust: to annihilate Ceto and Phorcys, it would have meant freeing the waters of evil and restoring serenity to the Ionius sea.

Meanwhile, Echidna, the sea monster that had left with Ladon, had come to the top of Lilybaeum and had sown terror among those peaceful territories inhabited by the Elymians, a population of fishermen and peasants. Those who had managed to save themselves had left for Krastos. Terrified men, women and children but fortunate to still be alive after having escaped the lethal and poisonous claws of the monster, were welcomed and cared for.

Word spread in the city of Krastos that Ladon had arrived at the eastern gate of the city and a reinforcement army had left to guard that area. Now the air was thick with tension.

Rosewood, deployed on the eastern walls was attentive to every slightest movement, but he didn't have to wait long for something to happen: the dawn of the new day showed in his eyes an elven army that galloped fast towards the fortified city. It was General Salix in retreat.

The doors were opened, and Salix and his silver elves flew in. Salix shouted orders in Elvish language, they were preparing for a frontal attack.

Rosewood left his post to go and greet his hawthorn's general.

"Salix what happened?"

The happiness of seeing him gave way to fear: he had never seen Salix so determined, he seemed almost wild even though he knew this was not possible. Perhaps he was worry about not being able to avoid other victims, he who possessed a high desire to protect the weakest.

"King Anax will soon arrive in Motyon and will surprise the black soldiers behind him. They will not understand that they will be finished until he is on them. A diversion of our bat friend will keep them occupied for the necessary time."

"Bats in attack I suppose … Eh, good the witch!" the leaf elf replied with a half-smile, pleased with what he had just heard.

"We will prepare to camouflage ourselves with the soil and vegetation, attacking them by surprise. King Corylus of the Green Valley of the Alcantara will descend from the north and will cover that side of the city, even arriving at Segesta, where, unfortunately, Echidna massacred the Elymians. The news came quickly, which is why I decided to act quickly. Rosewood, run to the Krastos' king, as our spokesman, and let him know about our plans: he will have to gather women, old people and children and go to the Old Mountain.After this you will come back to me, you will fight with us, like a valiant elf as you are."

Rosewood touched his lips and his heart as a promise to his general, then ran as fast as he could towards the royal palace. Salix gave orders all morning and slowly his army began to disappear outside the walls, camouflaging with the surrounding vegetation.

When Rosewood returned, he and Salix were the last to come out of the large armored door, vanishing like ghosts.

Abeius had arrived in Pantalica. He had decided to escort the princesses and Queen Vitalba home as promised to King Anax, but the valley seemed uninhabited. Everyone was frightened by the departure of their sovereign in the war, but as soon as the royal elves were recognized, the kingdom exploded in cheers; all welcomed the queen and princesses Daisy and Robinia, constantly giving thanks to Abeius for bringing them home.

But Abeius had to leave quickly, he left his delegation to Pantalica and vanished into confusion: he didn't even take his horse, nobody could intercept him on foot. Now he ran westward, on his way he saw the devastation left by the black army and the branchiere dogs: the dead were everywhere. His green eyes had never seen so much havoc, he felt the suffering of the earth on his skin, so many innocent deaths …

Too much blood had been spilled and still was not over, had this become the Trinacria, a land of death?

Chapter XXI

"Those islands in front of me seem to me … Watch out Typhoeus, they attack us!"

Tuia lowered her head to avoid a tail shot of a large red dragon.

"We will make them fly a little behind us and I will try to make them understand that we are visiting. I hope they soon recognize me as one of their breed. You hold on tight, now we are speeding!"

Typhoeus swooped down to a group of three huge green dragons and then went up again, flapping his large wings. Tuia, tied to the saddle, felt strong vibrations: it was her dragon that tried to communicate with the four beasts that pursued him. Finally, Typhoeus slowed his flight and so did the other four, together they began to descend to the coast.

From the upper Tuia could see the beauties of that magnificent land: myriads of birds flew over the greenery of that splendid island and already knew they were in that land that she had studied in her geography books and had always dreamed of: the green Ireland.

Typhoeus was escorted by the four huge dragons and, when they touched the ground, Tuia began to tremble in terror: the red dragon had come closer to peer at her and sniff her. Only when the elf felt Typhoeus's excitement, his happiness, she managed to calm down and tried to enjoy that miraculous event: his dragon had found his species believed to be extinct.

From far away a huge roar ripped through the air. Tuia winced, he must have been a huge beast. Typhoeus calmed Tuia by whispering: "It's Pendragon, the boss. Don't worry, he is a wise millennial dragon, we will talk to him, hoping he will accept to help us."

The golden dragon of Etna became majestic and solemn in front of that great chief who came to welcome him.

A giant and powerful red-eyed black dragon slowly approached. The vibrations of his body made Tuia tremble from head to toe, so much so that she tried to hide behind Typhoeus's big head. Concentrating, she realized that her dragon was conversing in Draconicus, the language of dragons, but she also understood that everything was going well because Typhoeus was strangely quiet.

"Come off the saddle and show you, my queen," Typhoeus told her seriously.

The young elf said nothing and obeyed; she was nervous and excited at the same time. Descending from the back of her golden dragon, she looked like a small ant compared to those huge winged beasts, they could have crushed her in a second without fussing.

Instead, Pendragon approached with his big head and inspected the elf from head to toe, lingering over the mark in the center of the golden armor.

"Elf, you carry the Triskelion branded on your chest."

The great black dragon spoke directly to Tuia and she was surprised by the fact that that dragon from Ireland knew the symbol of the Trinacria.

"Yes, because I belong to the island, to the Trinacria, and I must free it from those unclean monsters that devastate it."

"You are the last- born elf, the ogamic prophecy speaks of you. We will take you to those who have been waiting for your arrival for centuries. If the elven population becomes extinct on this island, our beloved and green Erin would also die."

Then he turned to Typhoeus: "We will take you to Ellan Vannin, the land of the tailless cats, a small island where the first elven generation still resides. If they do not start having descendants again … Dear little elf, only you are our hope."

Typhoeus made a sign to Tuia to get on his back and to tie herself up properly, they would fly very quickly to reach another small island nearby.

"Typhoeus, I'm so excited! What we are going to meet is an

ancient lineage from which the elves of our island come! Did Gabrys tell me, the bat witch who was born here, do you know her?"

Tuia was trembling, she never imagined she would go that far, her adventure was proving more fascinating than she thought.

"Of course, I know the bat. I hope, instead, that these elves don't remember me."

Typhoeus was annoyed by having to meet the elves whom he had damaged, he feared their resentment.

"Relax Typhoeus and enjoy the view."

Tuia was bewitched by the scenery that flowed beneath her: huge coasts and blue sea, everything shone under a bright morning sun and the green of those prairies entered her inside. She was also part of this world and she was proud of it.

Leaving the coast, Tuia and Typhoeus followed Pendragon that flew followed by the other four dragons, the three huge greens were near him while the fourth red dragon was behind them and occasionally approached to control the foreigners.

Pendragon landed before the others and approached a group of people near the coast who immediately ran inside a thick grove in front of the beach, where in the meantime all the other dragons were landing.

Several minutes passed, perhaps an hour. Tuia was entranced by those places, contemplating the sea, the coasts and the surrounding vegetation until an elegant delegation of elves came out of the thick forest carrying an emerald green banner where there was a symbol embroidered in gold.

"The Triskelion," Tuia murmured but had no way of saying other that all those elves knelt before her.

"We have been waiting for you for centuries, last-born elf, gift of the stars, to free us from the curse of sterility."

The elf who had spoken had to be the king of those ancient elves.

"Please stand up, I am so honored to meet you … The elves of the Trinacria belong to your lineage and for me, it is a great gift to make your acquaintance today."

Tuia blushed for so much reverence towards her.

"I am Orry, the king of Ellan Vannin, the island of the tailless cats. We have kept our ships ready waiting for the day when you would arrive, as an ancient prophecy tells. We are ready to fight and regain our honor. You came with the dragon that condemned us, but he has already paid with his suffering and has paid his debt to the elves bringing you to us. The wicked will succumb, and you will reconstitute the Triskelion to guarantee future generations to our people. When you give the order, we will leave "

King Orry bowed again and so did all the dragons, including Typhoeus who felt relieved by the words of the elven king. Tuia looked around dumbfounded for a moment, then gathered all the courage she had in her body and said:

"Get ready to go. The Trinacria is already under siege, invaded by the black soldiers of Adranos, by the sea monsters Ceto and Phorcys and by their unclean progeny. We have our future to save and too little time."

"Queen Tuia, Erin's dragons will follow you and fight at your side." Pendragon turned concerning an increasingly astonished Tuia. She hoped for nothing else.

"Let's go back to the green Erin, there will be some other scaly friend to be recruited."

Pendragon took to the air along with the other dragons while Tuia and Typhoeus waited to see the huge and light elven ships depart.

They climbed the coast and in a wide bay, they saw about ten wonderful ships, ready to set sail. The crew had waited centuries for the arrival of Tuia, that young elf bearer of hope, and now they were ready to return to Trinacria. From a distance, Tuia and Typhoeus saw the arrival of the king and his soldiers, while the Triskelion soared over every sail, over every armor and over every figurehead, where stood out the sculpture of a female elf. Tuia understood that the figureheads of the ten elven boats depicted her.

Tuia mounted on Typhoeus and flew on the sailing ships ready to sail. The captains of the ships waited for a nod from their much-desired elf. Typhoeus soared towards the clouds and plunged into the blue sea roaring and spitting fire; the Elven horns sounded all together, and the ships sailed, heading south behind the great golden dragon.

On the green coast of Erin, about ten dragons, headed by Pendragon, waited. As Typhoeus roared past the coast, they flew together and spit fire at the same time, following him like a flock of fearsome huge scaly birds.

Tuia turned to look, ten powerful dragons followed her, and on the sea, there was a fleet of splendid Elven ships. She felt proud of herself: she had her army too.

Chapter XXII

Great and fearsome armies were on their way: on the one hand the good for the defense of the life of the Trinacria, on the other the power-hungry evil to conquer the island.

The young Galateia had come to Selinos. For a while, she had left the horse offered by the elves to continue on foot and hide in some river or small stream. Approaching the coast where the temple of the Gorgons stood could be dangerous, she did not know where Echidna and Ladon had come from and what other horrors they had already committed besides those already seen.

Silently she approached the valley of the temples of the city of Selinos, where the largest and most elegant home of the Gorgons stood. Huge and powerful monolithic columns formed their refuge, chosen to hide and honor the head of the most dangerous of the monstrous sisters: Medusa.

No one lived in those parts or perhaps they had all fled: the houses were empty, and the streets were deserted, around them there was only desolation.

From the coast, you could admire the sea and the sunset that gave a touch of orange all around, warm and surreal, but Galateia had to find the courage to enter.

Curled up next to the entrance as old blankets there were the Graeae, the two monstrous witches with one eye who were there to guard access to the temple of the Gorgons. Galateia had to go around them without being seen. She stood awhile looking at them from behind a huge boulder. They were shriveled and dirty like ragged rags, with a horrible red eye that passed between their hands, constantly bickering like two acidic wives.

Galateia decided to do as her father Nereus suggested. She approached silently the enormous column where the two old witches sat, intent on quarreling as usual for those who should have the privilege of keeping the precious eye, picked up a handful of soil and dust from the ground and in the click of a second threw it at the blood-red creepy eyeball.

The two monsters began to scream and curse the wind that had blinded them, not recognizing that behind that event there could be someone else. Galateia smiled and without making any noise went past the screaming old women and entered the temple of the Gorgons. She crossed the six huge stone columns, climbed the steps, then passed through another colonnade. The light from outside filtered little, making it almost impossible to see anything, then the interior suddenly lit up, millions of candles lit up, and Nereus's young daughter could finally make out what she had in front of her: two huge braziers and in the middle, an altar, where the decapitated head of a sleeping Medusa lay on a gilded pillow.

Galateia had never seen anything more horrible: the huge head had a mass of live snakes as hair that watched and protected it, she only hoped it wouldn't open its eyes.

Suddenly, however, she heard two voices that seemed to come straight out of the underworld.

"Cousin, what brings you out of the sea to face your worst nightmare?"

Stheno and Euryale, the two Gorgons, had appeared quietly from behind a column and approached the altar of Medusa.

"I greet you … dear cousins … I am here … Well, courage … Ceto and Phorcys have stolen the thoughts of the elf Tuia and I have managed to steal the sphere of thoughts and bring it here so that Medusa can guard it, as the oracle of the Cathedral cave revealed to my father."

Galateia was panting after saying it all in one breath, without breathing.

The two female figures, wrapped in black cloaks, turned to the altar and moved slowly to feed the fires.

"We have been here for some time, feared and hated, we have lost our beloved sister and we will watch over it forever. Nobody saved her, not even those horrible monsters called parents, they didn't even save us from our terrible endless curse. This is our life, but it will also be the end of those who will desecrate our temple by becoming stone to our gaze, just as the hearts that condemned us were made of stone."

One of the two sisters lowered the black hood revealing a head of slimy and hissing snakes, while the other one that was still busy on the altar, showing bronze hands spoke:

"You are here today, giving us a chance for revenge on our parents and we will be grateful to you forever. This is why we will give you the chance to come out alive of the encounter with the fearsome Gorgons."

With an almost whispered voice, the second sister had raised a bit of terror from the young Nereid, then she too let her hood slip on her shoulders, showing the same reptiles as hair. Again, Galateia was overcome with despair, all she wanted to do was get away from that cursed place.

Both the Gorgons began to approach Galateia walking backward so as not to petrify her with their eyes, but the nereid could barely manage not to give in to terror.

Stheno and Euryale stopped about a meter from Galateia, then whispered: "Give us the green sphere of thoughts."

Nereus's young daughter trembled from head to toe. She took the precious sphere out of her bag of seaweed and stretched her arm as far as she could. The Gorgons barely turned, grabbed the sphere and quickly headed for the altar where the horrible head of Medusa awoke instantly: her terrible red eyes opened, and the snakes stirred, grabbing the ball and wrapping it with their coils. The sphere lit up with a bright green and then went out like a crown on the decapitated head of the fearful Gorgon.

"Go away, your mission is accomplished. Remember, only the elf to whom the thoughts belong can claim what is hers, otherwise, they will remain with us forever."

That said, Stheno and Euryale threw a green powder on the braziers and a thick black smoke expanded inside the temple. Galateia escaped with raised legs towards the outside.

"Well, well what are you doing in these parts Nereus's daughter? Echidna had climbed from the coast and had blocked Galateia in a second while trying to escape away from the temple of the Gorgons.

"I saw you come in and now you're out, still alive … how and why?"

The monster's grip was firm and powerful, and the nereid could do nothing to free herself but did not speak. She looked at the sea hoping that someone would come soon to rescue her.

Meanwhile, Motyon had been besieged, the witch's diversion Gabrys with her bats had given the hawthorn's armies time to retreat within the walls of Krastos and to organize the counterattack from the most fortified city in the entire Trinacria. Inico and Mozio, the generals of the Sicans and Elymians, knew that at least two thousand elves of the hawthorn were hidden in front of the fortress.

It was sunset, a blood-red tinged the sky, the volcanic eruption of Etna was the background to that waiting scenario. Would King Anax hit the black army in Motyon? Would they have succeeded in doing it? Elven horns could be heard in the distance: beyond the Hymera river, they fought again. The army of the kingdom of Pantalica had arrived in Motyon and already clashed with the black men of Adranos, the sound of blows and the screams of battle echoed in the Sicans mountains, on the Madonie and the Nebrodi, the whole island trembled.

Abeius scanned the valley from the Erei mountains and noticed the arrival of the most dangerous army he had ever seen, headed by the evilest person on the island, Adranos.

He ran as fast as he could, had to arrive on time to warn King Anax, or Adranos would hit him in the back.

Motyon stood out in front of him, a battlefield where men, elves and dogs clashed violently while a huge monster similar to a large reptile horrified anyone who happened to be in its clutches, it was the terrible Ladon. Abeius stood in front of it, every muscle in his body vibrating with tension, now Ladon was his and it would die by his sword.

"You, hideous gnat, how dare you! Would you like to hit me? You will all die, worms of the earth, all the elves will die, and we will finally recover the island!"

Ladon screamed like a beast hungry against the elf, but nothing it could do against the agility of Abeius who jumped on it and thrust the sword into its neck. The horrendous monster's eyes bulged and lifeless fell to the ground.

"I hate that my land must absorb the poisonous blood of this being … But we approach the Triskelion, dear Tuia."

With the thought of his precious elf in his head, he ran to King Anax to warn him of the arrival of King Adranos and his army, but he did not have time to discuss with him a possible strategy that from the forest came out him, the black king.

Charging, mowing anyone who was on his way followed by an evil horde that galloped towards Krastos, unstoppable: Adranos wanted to storm the fortress city, he had to conquer it.

The branchiere dogs massacred the poor wounded on the pavement while the elves tried to eliminate the ferocious beasts to prevent them to devour the soldiers. It was a terrifying scenario, King Anax and his soldiers fought relentlessly. Then at the last light of sunset came King Corylus and the elves of the Green Valley of Alcantara.

They descended from the mountains to give support to the allies, now the two kings were two lions and black soldiers and dogs fell under the swords and elven bows.

Abeius had resumed his role as a general, had recalled his army of hawks and resumed his chase in pursuit of Adranos: Krastos could not fall.

The elves of King Corylus were real war machines, trained to the sword and hand-to-hand combat, muscular and lethal like real peregrine falcons hunting for prey; but they hunted the wicked and were ready to face the race and the fight because they were masters of resistance and tactics.

Abeius was proud to be the general of such perfect companions and now no one could stop him with his men beside him. He had not seen Salix, but he knew his talents as a good strategist and thought he had organized a tactical retreat. He hoped with all of himself that he would soon identify his strategy.

Krastos was near and already Adranos had begun to hit the walls with his war machines, driven by Ceto and Phorcys who had climbed the Kalikos river and had come out in front of the fortified city ready to serve the evil black king.

As soon as Abeius and his hawks sprouted beyond the jungle, thousands of elves began to launch their arrows; it was not known where they came from, but it was sure they came to the mark: the black soldiers fell under the elf phantom attack. General Salix's strategy was proving productive.

From under the ground the roots of the trees clung and pulled down the men: it seemed that nature was rebelling against all that destruction. Rosewood had awakened the trees and commanded the camouflaged attack in the bark of a huge oak. Even if the losses were huge, the elves would have won.

Abeius fought and his army was ready to stop only at the end when the elves would have won. Even the elves of the hawthorn did their part, camouflaged among the vegetation they killed a black soldier behind the other, as their general foresaw.

Ceto and Phorcys operated the catapults and supported huge staircases to let the soldiers enter the city, on the fortified walls the generals of the men, Elymians and Sicans, fought tirelessly to defend it but the black army was clearly superior in number.

A small hole was opened in the doorway. They fought while fiery boulders passed the ramparts and hit the inside of Krastos. The city walls had given way.

Adranos with his banners ran to the great royal palace, he screamed and enjoyed watching the city that was falling under his feet, wildly excited, sure that he would rule the island.

The sunset light was fading, but a distant glow became stronger and more insistent: it was the volcanic eruption of Etna and Tuia and Typhoeus knew very well that they were close.

Then turning to the west, they saw distant fumes and flames; the war was on and they had to hurry.

In Draconic, Typhoeus spoke to the dragons flying behind him and they all turned west to glide over the battlefield.

"Are you ready, my friend? The time has come."

"Yes, my queen."

The dragons formed a circle above the battlefield and, after identifying the enemies, they launched down quickly.

Typhoeus began to spit fire on the black army, the other dragons glided and devoured the dogs that had the ardor to attack them, others fled away in fear of those enormous winged beasts. Even the black soldiers, those few remaining alive, fled in terror and the city of Motyon, or what was left of it, was soon released.

Tuia looked around, and when she saw that by now no one was fighting, she came down from her dragon and ran towards the two kings. She already knew King Anax but was intimidated by the mighty appearance of the king of the Green Valley of the Alcantara: he looked like an imposing tree, perhaps the largest that could exist on earth. Dark and deep eyes, serious and honest, long black hair and that tanned complexion she had already noticed in Abeius, King Corylus was a good giant. King Anax, on the other hand, had more elegant and gentle features, a lighter complexion, blue eyes, and blond hair. The elves of both kingdoms of the Trinacria took the characteristics of the territories they inhabited, the elves of Pantalica being more luminous and fluid, like the water of the river, sturdy and dark like oak and chestnut, but powerful as the Etna the elves of Alcantara Green Valley. The first smelled of flowers and aromatic herbs, the others of hazelnut, apple and forest.

As soon as Tuia approached, she immediately noticed the difference between the two, but both Elven kings looked at her gently and greeted her with reverence as if she was a great queen.

"Young Tuia we thank you and honor the dragons."

King Anax and King Corylus expressed themselves in the same way and both their respective armies knelt to honor Tuia and the majestic dragons.

Tuia had not yet become accustomed to these manifestations

towards her and blushed, the dragons instead appreciated the thanks of the elven people, especially Pendragon.

With her bright green eyes, the young Greener peered at the battlefield, dared not look between the bodies on the ground, but wished to see her generals Abeius and Salix.

King Anax read the anxiety in her eyes and said: "Little Tuia they are in Krastos, to defend the city with the rest of our armies, with the Elymians and the Sicans. Unfortunately, Adranos is already there and has an unstoppable army, but with the dragons, we can win."

King Anax and King Corylus after talking, got on their horses and headed for the city, ready to resume fighting for their island.

"Adranos is already there!"

Tuia to that revelation of the king of the hawthorn remained dazed, she never imagined seeing him so soon. Her mind was racing: what effect would meeting him have?

Her gaze fell on a man squirming on the ground, then on another and a third. She noticed that there were so many survivors, many dying, and a great pain suddenly caught her.

"Tuia is your moment, fire water will heal them."

Typhoeus urged Tuia to act quickly, the young elf took from the saddlebag of the dragon's saddle the ampoules of the Palics that the flames had filled with the tears of Typhoeus and began to leap from one wounded soldier to another, trying to save as many people as possible, enemies and friends, dripping a drop of that miraculous water to each of the wounded soldiers.

She found herself in front of dead elves and her heart tore from pain, then she saw the agony in the lifeless face of an enemy, one of those dreaded black men and she understood that death was the same for everyone. For a moment she lost herself in despair, she needed to cry and vent her pain in front of all that horror.

All of a sudden, she heard herself call: "Tuia, come."

Pendragon showed her a group of Branchiere dogs, brutally wounded who had crawled and hidden among the brambles, trying to alleviate their suffering by licking each other.

Tuia was terrified by that vision: those were lethal beasts. Pendragon whispered to her: "Bring love where it never was."

Tuia gathered all the courage she had and slowly approached the large injured dogs. No one snarled or tried to bite her, and she managed to drop a drop of fire water in each of those dangerous jaws. Immediately the wounds were healed, and the elf had a moment of panic, surrounded by huge dangerous and healthy beasts. Then a big dog came up to her and licked her hand.

Like a docile puppy, it was a warm kiss of thanks.

"See Tuia? Love works miracles."

Pendragon was proud of the courage she had shown.

The herd of dogs fled away, but before they disappeared, they stopped on a hill and howled together towards Krastos, under a huge newly birth moon.

Krastos fought relentlessly, the city was under siege and elves, men and dogs fought fiercely. All of a sudden, the Branchieres who were intent on fighting against their enemies stopped, looked at the moon and left Krastos to go east, where they had been called back. No one could have imagined such a thing, a sigh of relief reached the Elven armies, especially for the Sicans and the Elymians who were terrorized by large molossers.

Tuia thought that the dogs had howled like wolves or because they were happy to be saved, and kept checking around if anyone else needed firewater. The wounds of the sea monsters were poisonous and lethal, those who were still alive were lucky to receive the miraculous elixir of Tuia, because in no other case would they have been saved.

After about half an hour, from thc west, it was heard as the roar of a cavalry. The dragons shielded the survivors and Tuia mounted Typhoeus ready to fly away in case of danger. From the hillside appeared a thousand running dogs, a dangerous herd going eastward: they had been recalled by the dogs saved by the elf.

"They return to their home. They will go free in the Nebrodi mountains, where they were born, to enjoy their freedom. See Tuia, a simple act of compassion has created the conditions necessary to beat Adranos, because doing good can only bring other good."

Typhoeus was really happy. Pendragon looked at Tuia and she saw an appreciation in his eyes towards her; it was the first time that she really felt proud of herself. She had never felt this way, and this made her feel really good.

After the last branchiere had disappeared in the middle of the woods, the dragons chatted a little between them, then Typhoeus said: "We are ready, my little flame."

"Let's go win this war. To Krastos!"

Tuia raised her sword high and all the dragons roared and took flight at once.

From the top, the siege was clearly visible. The sky was dark, by now it was evening and the smoke had made the air hot and unbreathable; houses burned, fields burned, the ten dragons landed fearsome on the battlefield and began to spit fire on the army of Adranos, who at the sight of the enormous beasts began to slip away and flee towards the hills.

Outside walls had been demolished, the battle was now taking place inside the fortress city and the flag of Adranos towered over the royal palace.

Tuia and Typhoeus flew over the palace leaving the rest of the dragons to fight with the elves of King Corylus and King Anax. Krastos would have been deserted if there had been no militias in combat.

Tuia tried to see Abeius or Salix, but it was impossible from that height, she had to go ashore.

She was really angry about the bad situation found in Krastos: Adranos had put the entire city on fire and it totally burned. She decided to go down to the tower where she had seen his black flag-waving with that Branchiere's red-head that stood out threateningly.

"He must be inside. I want to face him in person." Tuia had decided that the Sicel king had to die by her hand, he had to pay for all the harm he had caused.

"We will go down into the inner courtyard of the building. The smoke has wound to the towers, I'm sure we'll find that vile of Adranos there." That said Typhoeus veered and descended into the palace gardens. Everywhere there were men fighting. The hawks of King Corylus were distinguished because they literally mowed down their enemies, they were tall and muscular, and the black soldiers succumbed to their strength. Then there were arrows that you couldn't tell where they came from, but they always went to target.

Then there he was: Abeius delivering powerful and deadly sword strokes, to whom? Adranos.

Finally, Tuia saw him for the first time. The black king had savage wickedness painted on his face, he was possessed, and bloodthirsty. He wore a black metal bust with a dog red-head in the center, surrounded by red to make the animal more threatening, that was what the Sicel king wanted, to terrorize anyone in front of him.

"Die dirty insect! You and all the other annoying gnats like you will die, I will rid the island of your infestation and I will be the absolute king!"

Adranos screamed, striking at an Abeius who managed to block him but not without difficulty: the pact with the evil monsters had given Adranos an unnatural force.

"Today you will die, damn you! You will pay for the deaths and suffering you have caused on this island!"

Tuia's voice tore at the air, as she approached slowly, her face transfigured by anger, with her sword drawn ready to fight the one who had made her island unlivable.

"Go away!" screamed Abeius at her, terrified that the Sicel king could hurt her.

"No, Abeius, you will be the one to retreat. This is my battle and I'm here to punish him for what he did. I want him to perish under my sword. Even Typhoeus will not interfere, it's a family matter … Isn't it?"

A sour smile stood out on the face of the young Greener who hurled herself, with all the strength she was wearing, onto Adranos. The man was surprised to see her and he was surprised by her power particularly.

Tuia and Adranos fought and struck each other. She was able to block the blows inflicted by the black king, but she felt them violent and strong. She faltered, then heard a voice coming from afar, beyond time, perhaps from another world or perhaps only from within her:

"Tuia you can do it. Fight my daughter, believe in what you are, believe in yourself."

The voice was that of Mr Carlo: her father encouraged her as he had always done. His words resounded in her soul, while she was there to face yet another powerful sword strike inflicted by Adranos.

"Dad!" Tuia screamed in amazement, unable to understand where the sound of her human dad's voice might have come from, a voice so dear from one of the few that she would have liked to have near in all that absurd story.

Adranos froze, he was dumbfounded and confused for a moment, but that was enough for Tuia to grab her two-handed sword and strike a powerful blow that dropped the weapon to the black king, who had been left looking at her upset. Now she was there with her sword in her hand and her enemy on the ground, disturbed, in silence, staring at her with wide eyes.

"You called me Dad …" the black king said in a faint voice.

"I will never call you dad, you just deserve to die!" the young elf replied cold and angry, screaming.

"You called me daddy," repeated Adranos, more and more puzzled.

"No!"

A chilling scream came out of Tuia's lungs and arrived

everywhere. The earth trembled and the air vibrated, the Etna imploded and whoever remained to fight inside Krastos stopped to look at the black king, sovereign of the Sicels, on the ground, at the feet of the young Tuia holding a big sword of black metal, ready to skewer him. For a few seconds, everything was silent. Elves, Elymians and Sicans, black soldiers and dragons, all waiting for Tuia's action silently, then a woman screamed: "Everyone on the ground!"

It was the witch Gabrys who had grabbed Abeius and thrown him on the pavement.

Etna exploded inside Tuia, the eruption made her a glowing ball of fire. A voice from the deepest caverns of the volcano spoke:

"You wicked man, with your cruelty you have made this land touch suffering and violence, you deserve to die. You have destroyed many lives and in others, you have brought terror by allying yourself with the worst beings of this earth. I am here today to fulfill my mission."

"I hated that race that took you away from me. If I had to suffer, everyone else had to suffer. I lost my family and my honor at the same time that the elves took you away … You were my powerful heir."

The more he spoke, the more King Adranos seemed to shrink under the weight of his words, especially in front of Tuia, which had become as fiery as Etna's lava.

"Calm down Tuia …" Typhoeus whispered.

"Don't tell me what to do, he's the culprit of all this."

The volcano spoke through her, it wanted its revenge, and now its anger had reached the maximum power.

While the world seemed to have stopped to observe the fiery elf, the monsters Ceto and Phorcys entered the city to go and help their ally and the black soldiers. Encouraged by that apparent calm they approached bold and arrogant, convinced that they could finally complete their evil mission.

"Elf, finally we meet!"

Ceto turned to Tuia, thinking he could catch her or even kill her, but he didn't have time to get close.

"How dare you?" said the voice of Etna. The incandescent elf turned and hurled the larger meteors she'd ever created at the two monsters, incinerating them instantly.

Everyone threw themselves on the ground with their hands on their heads. Adranos covered his head thinking that the third ball of fire was for him, but it didn't arrive. It seemed that everything was over until a third monster appeared from behind the ruins of the surrounding wall. It was Echidna who showed Galateia clutching her in deadly claws.

"Elf! I will avenge my brothers and your lineage will end, I will begin with her, so you will understand who you are dealing with."

Arrogant Echidna showed the poor Nereid fainted, shaking her violently.

"Let her go and I will give you time to reach the sea so to never see yourself again."

So spoke the voice of the volcano.

Echidna was terrified by the tone and words uttered by the fiery elf, so it threw poor Galateia defenseless towards Tuia and fled towards the coast. From a tree came a very fast figure that grabbed the young Nereid before she could fall to the ground: it was General Salix who until then had remained camouflaged with his soldiers among the trees of the forest that surrounded the city of Krastos.

From the coast, you could see a huge wave that rose from the sea as soon as Echidna dived into it. To the reflections of the burning fire of Krastos you could realize that the sea boiled, that something was happening among those furious waves, but the darkness didn't allow to see beyond.

Typhoeus approached Tuia and blew on her face. The elf fell unconscious, a powerful shake shook the whole island and Etna erupted again in all its magnificence: its spirit had returned to the deep meanders of the volcano and Tuia had resumed her appearance as a young elf red-haired.

Abeius picked her up and kissed her on the forehead, relieved to see her still alive. She slowly opened her eyes, she smelled her dear Abeius, so she raised an arm and squeezed him tightly around his neck.

"It's all over, baby, you beat the black king." Abeius whispered softly as he placed her gently under a large fir tree.

Tuia looked up, smiled and said, "Abeius resembles you."

A slight growl came from Typhoeus's throat that followed the scene with a little jealousy.

The black soldiers had vanished, many had fled as soon as they saw the dragons coming, others when they realized that their king had lost power. Everyone had returned to their countries, perhaps now they would live as free men, returning to their families.

The generals of the two elven peoples climbed the highest tower of the great palace of Krastos and blew into two large horns to announce to the whole island and to the people who had taken refuge in the Old Mountain that the war had ended. Mozio and Inico embraced moved, the city had almost been razed to the ground, but together the two peoples would have rebuilt in peace, serenity and brotherhood.

"Rosewood! Rosewood … where are you?" Desperate Gabrys was looking for her little leaf elf, the smoke had cleared up and all the elves of the hawthorn had by now become visible, to the roll call lacked only Rosewood. Frightened Tuia started looking for him everywhere, then heard Typhoeus calling her:

"Is this the leaf elf you are looking for? He had fainted on that smoked oak."

The golden dragon had gently taken and placed him under the fir tree where Tuia had been placed. Gabrys, Tuia and Abeius ran to see how he was, the young Greener had prepared the ampoule with the firewater, but as soon as she moved to cure him, Gabrys yelled at her:

"Stop! Don't do it, you could kill him! Water of fire, tells you anything? No, for him a little water from the Kalikos river will be good."

Someone already came with a bowl of fresh water; it was Salix who from a distance had followed the scene of the discovery of Rosewood and he had immediately given himself to do.

"Thank you, general." Gabrys was really grateful for such diligence. With a cold shower, he hit the Rosewood face that opened his eyes immediately.

"Oh, I finally breathe! The smoke was killing me … Thanks for this bucket full of life."

Then he looked around and said: "I knew we would have won, even if in my humble opinion I could have fought on my own … maybe with some elf, one, two not more."

"Instead, thank Tuia for bringing the dragons, making the black soldiers flee and beating Adranos."

Salix pointed out.

"I knew it, I knew it would be you! You could already see from your habit that you were a winner, a beautiful warrior, the maximum that …"

"Oh, Rosewood and that's it! Where did you put the little pipino that I gave you? Why didn't you use it to call me? I thought you were dead, pungent little nettle leaf …"

Gabrys blurted, but this made everyone laugh, including the leaf elf who had discovered that he had forgotten to own the little pipino Gabrys had given him before leaving for Krastos. With a somewhat guilty but smiling face, he showed it to everyone, but the witch tore it quickly from his hands and angrily went away, leaving the little leaf elf surprised.

It was dawning, a new, peaceful sun, welcoming Elymians and Sicans, the elves of King Corylus and King Anax, while the population of Krastos slowly returned from the Old Mountain. All were welcomed and embraced, relieved to see the faces of fathers and husbands, battered but alive, all gathered around the large square of Krastos, where, in the center, the black king Adranos chained had been placed in logs.

As soon as the sun came up everyone started whispering: "Palikè,

Palikè, Palikè."

In unison men and elves revealed their decision to the sun. Gabrys moved near the prisoner. Tuia did not understand what all this strange ceremony meant, then the bat turned to her:

"Dearest Tuia, you will decide his destiny: as you have heard, elves and men want him to go to Palikè and be tried by the Palics at the Naftia ponds. Since you are now the queen of the Sicels, as the sole heir to the throne and by right of conquest, you can decide whether Adranos, the black king, deserves a trial or death for your sword."

Again, Tuia felt her anger rising.

"I am not his heir … I am not his daughter!"

Adranos raised his head and looked at the young elf in her beautiful green eyes and dared to speak to her again:

"I declared you my only and legitimate heir when I first picked you up, then to seal the pact between elves and men, I signed a will where you would be the only one able to govern once my death occurred. Then those cursed elves took you away, they held you and then my kingdom. That was why I decided to make a pact of immortality with the terrible sea monsters, if I was not dead, my kingdom would never have passed to these gnats. If you had been by my side … we could have governed the entire island with the power of fire."

Adranos was staring insistently at Tuia as he spoke, as if in defiance, as if to tell her that everything he had done up to that point had been her fault and that of the elven people.

Tuia tried to contain her anger, but she had to respond to that wicked and evil being in front of her:

"Don't try to misrepresent the facts, you did it because you were a cowardly and fearful king: you feared that the elves had left you alone to fight the Phoenicians and, since they had taken away your precious and powerful little elf, you betrayed them. You are just a vile traitor, you let King Corylus fight your war alone and then introduce yourself with that abominable rabble as allies. You wanted to kill your wife too, to seal that monstrous union with

Ceto and Phorcys, but she decided, in her great pain of betrayed wife and suffering mother, to give her soul to the volcano. You brought too much pain on this island; you deserve to die."

Tuia was a river in flood and the words boiled inside.

"Thalia …" Adranos murmured in surprise as if he remembered only at that moment to have had a wife.

"You have no right to name that woman!" I should kill you instantly … You deserve to die for how you killed thousands of people! Have you looked at all those dead men in the face? No, right? I saw them: men who fought for your thirst for power and died and killed others just for your greed … What monster is the man who becomes powerful on the suffering of others, on the helpless? You managed to poison even the lives of those dogs, the dogs that are among the most loyal animal to man … You managed to make them ruthless and murderous.

No, I will not kill you, you are so unworthy that you do not deserve to even perish under my sword … That he is brought to Palikè."

The general exultation was opposed to the disapproval of Abeius, but the general knew that Tuia was right.

Then the young Greener spoke again, but this time it turned to the elves:

"I was on the island of Ellan Vannin and there I met the elven people we came from, the ones who left the island after the destruction of the Triskelion. They left with their ships and are arriving in Trinacria."

The elves were incredulous, very happy to finally be free of the curse of sterility, because the arrival of the northern people, according to an ogamic prophecy, meant that the anathema could be dissolved.

Gabrys was the happiest of all, screaming like a madman in the sky:

"At home, at home! I will finally come back to my house!"

Then she saw Tuia who had darkened and left the square. Gabrys ran behind her suspiciously and went down to the beach. The sea was beautiful and shone in the morning sun, it seemed made of shimmering crystals.

The young elf was crying.

"Little star of fire, we celebrate and you cry, what troubles you now?"

Gabrys pulled back the red hair from Tuia's face and saw her green eyes filled with tears.

"I couldn't complete my mission … Where is the Triskelion? How am I going to put it back together if I have incinerated the monsters I needed to rebuild it. Their limbs were needed, do you understand? I didn't succeed in anything … The little human Tuia will sleep unconsciously all her life and I will not have accomplished anything of what I was created for … I failed."

Gabrys looked at those tears of Tuia's sorrow, as sincere as the waters of the sea that bathed her feet, then wiped them off, took her face, and looking into her eyes then she said:

"You are the most precious soul we have on this island, remember that. If there is an air of celebration today it is thanks to you. It is thanks to you if we have succeeded in annihilating the evil that oppressed us and then you are bringing back to me my dear Orry, he will not believe to see me again and this time he will have to take me as a wife, for all the prickly pears!"

Now Gabrys was smiling and the shadow of a slight smile also appeared on Tuia's face.

"Now let's go, everyone expects to see you smiling."

The witch took Tuia by the shoulders and climbed the sandy coast, going back to the square, where elves and men danced and they celebrated together.

An evil laugh rose from the center of the square, it was the black king who scornfully derided the elves.

"Celebrate, gnats?" Too bad, your relatives won't come here! At the Cape Pelorus, Scylla and Charybdis are waiting for them, your beloved friends will drown in the straits or be devoured by those terrible jaws!"

Tuia looked at terrified Adranos, Gabrys blanched to hear that atrocious revelation, and the whole square fell into a grave silence, then she resolute said:

"The war is not over, Abeius to the dragons with me."

Tuia was determined to kill the island's last monsters and would do so with Abeius at her side.

The hawks' general ran to meet her, but first, he approached Adranos and gave him a powerful punch in the face.

"Damn you, you'd already been dead if that was up to me," he yelled two inches from his bleeding nose.

The two elves were running fast on the hill where the dragons basked in the warm late August sun, as soon as they saw them from afar, they rose, the scales shining like precious gems. Typhoeus gleamed more than the sun, Pendragon seemed made of black crystal, then there was an elegant red dragon that seemed to be set with rubies and the other seven green dragons, wonderful and sparkling like emeralds.

Tuia ran directly to Typhoeus, who immediately got her on the saddle, explaining what was happening on the other side of the island. Abeius hesitated a moment, but Pendragon grabbed him gently and placed him on his spine: he had chosen his knight. Tuia's heart swelled with emotion, her general would have ridden the dragon leader.

"Wha … what should I do?" The hawks' general asked in a thin voice.

"Hold on tight!" said Tuia, Typhoeus, and Pendragon together. The take-off was fast and impetuous, they had to get to Cape Pelorus before it was too late. Tuia knew the chilling legends about Scylla and Charybdis and was terrified of what might have happened.

The Trinacria from above looked wonderful. While the dragons flew over the Sicans mountains, Tuia could see from above the fields of golden wheat that shone in the sun, the red of tomatoes and the green of watermelons. Vineyards and prickly pears, orange and lemon trees … nothing was missing from her island, just a little peace and serenity and she would have done everything to give it to it.

They routed further north, flying over the Madonie and Nebrodi mountains ranges. Now to their left, you could see the blue expanse of the Tyrrenous Sea. Not even the shadow of the ten elven ships from Ireland; Tuia was really worried, they should already have been close, and could already be under siege by Scylla and Charybdis.

"We hope not to have arrived too late." Tuia expressed her concern to Typhoeus.

"We will arrive on time, I promise you."

Typhoeus began to flap his wings furiously, accelerating. The other dragons did the same and finally managed to see the Elven ships stuck on the strait. Scylla and Charybdis were intent on throwing huge boulders at the vessels, the elves defended themselves as they could by throwing their arrows, but they had been surprised by an ambush and were not ready to face such an enemy.

Even Scylla and Charybdis were taken by surprise by the dragons who fell on them with claws and jaws, savagely tearing them as Tuia had never seen before. The monstrous marine beasts tried to defend themselves as they could using deadly limbs, but the Irish dragons left them no escape. Tuia and Abeius flew over the ships to check that no one had been injured or killed: some ships had already suffered damage, but all in all they had arrived on time. Only a few shreds remained of Scylla and Charybdis, and Abeius picked up a limb from each monster. He wrapped them in a torn sail: they could be used to reassemble the Triskclion, even if he was already beginning to have some doubts about their real utility, but he never mentioned it to Tuia.

After checking the ships, the elves resumed sailing, escorted by Tuia and Abeius to the port of Naxos, where the local population, the Sicels, greeted them amicably and made them rest and refresh before resuming their journey to the bay of Krastos.

Tuia looked at those people and was really happy to have released them from their king's wickedness, even the castle of Naxos seemed less dark to her now. The Etna in the background had found peace and only a light smoke escaped from the huge crater, just to signal that it was there, always vigilant.

Tuia greeted "A Muntagna" with a nod of the head and left to return to Krastos: she still had to take care of Adranos and understand how she could recompose the Triskelion since she lacked a limb.

She thought it might be that of the Echidna monster, maybe he could even go looking for it to kill it. But who knows where he had fled … why had she let it go?

Chapter XXIII

Krastos from the top looked devastated, the rubble still smoked. It was sad and distressing to see a city, which must have been marvelous, reduced to ashes. The thing that struck Tuia the most, however, was the joy of the people, the desire to start over, and the enthusiasm to rebuild: everyone had waited for the return of the young Greener to celebrate, and a very long table had been created with the fallen boards of some houses to make a banquet worthy of a king, or rather three kings, who toasted Tuia all the time.

Tuia could not be completely happy, what mission had she completed? None.

She got up from the table and went to sit on the beach, watching the crystalline waves of the sea. She loved the smell of those waters and began to caress them following the movement of the waves, then a hand came out and grabbed hers. Looking up, she met two other deep green eyes.

"Dear Tuia, what makes you sad? I am Nereus, the sage of the sea. I am here to thank you for saving my daughter, my sweet and courageous Galateia."

The old man of the sea turned his gaze to the beach, where Tuia could see a beautiful young girl walking hand in hand with "her" Salix.

"Well, I see that the young Galateia has woken up … Hello Nereus, you are also a Greener from what I can see. Anyway, do you know what makes me sad? Having failed my mission on the Triskelion and not being able to save the little human Tuia, do you realize? And in the city, some people even toast in my honor!" Tuia explained, shifting her gaze from the new pair of lovers to the face of the elderly gentleman in front of her.

"Yes dear, I am a guardian like you, my element is water and I know where the sphere of thoughts of the little human is hidden."

Nereus smiled as if he had made a small prank. Tuia jumped to her feet in disbelief. She hoped he wasn't kidding. "Really, are you sure?"

"Of course, I put it there! No, it's not correct … Galateia made the journey to secure the green sphere that is now in Selinos at the temple of the Gorgons, under Medusa's surveillance."

The old man of the sea gave a smile as if he had won some kind of prize.

Tuia instead shuddered. "Medusa?! You're joking, right?"

"No, no. The oracle of the Cathedral cave told me to bring the sphere there and that you are the only one able to recover it: only the legitimate owner can do it." Nereus kept smiling.

"But couldn't this oracle do his business? Or maybe tell you to take it directly to me. Instead, no … Medusa! Do you realize?!"

Tuia started pacing back and forth, muttering, imitating Gabrys when she was nervous.

"By the way… Since you live in these waters, isn't it that you've come across Echidna lately? I have to find it and, just because I like easy things, I should amputate it a limb … Maybe you know its address."

By now Tuia was at the highest levels of nervousness, trying to dampen the moment with a sour irony.

"Oh … Well, actually Echidna made a bad end last night. I and my marine army, if we can call it sharks, dolphins, orcas, and all the inhabitants of the sea, we waited for Ceto and Phorcys to appear. We waited hidden in the waves and from there we also admired the bonfire you made of them … You were superb, among other things. Then Echidna arrived and you let him go …"

"Come on, turn the knife in the wound again …" Tuia snorted, lowering her gaze nervously.

"Anyway, that damned guy who had dared to abuse my daughter headed straight for the sharks … What end do you think it did?" now Nereus was laughing at thirty-two teeth.

Tuia put her hands over her face to hide the ugly expression that had come to her, discovering that nothing was left of Echidna. Nereus said goodbye to her, crushing her in a strong embrace, and disappeared again in the waves as he had arrived.

Tuia stared at the void, her ears whistling and her mind whirling like a grinder:

"The green sphere, Medusa, Selinos, Medusa, Echidna … Oh, but one foot they could leave me … I have to talk to Gabrys and Abeius … and then go to Selinos and try again to sell my skin dangerously."

She went up thoughtfully a sandy hill that led from the beach to the city but she often turned to look at the sea. Not far away, two figures sat on the sand, very close together: Salix and the nereid Galateia. They seemed to be in love … who knows if she had lost herself in his wonderful blue eyes or in his sweet perfume, who knows if her heart had made a thousand somersaults like when she had discovered that the general of the hawthorn would be her bow's teacher.

Perhaps in such situation, she should have felt pain, but too many things had happened and, in reality, it was fine even so.

Not far away, Typhoeus, lying in the sun near the wonderful red dragon, was watching her. He had understood the strange situation in which Tuia's soul felt, but he had decided that she had to manage to solve her torments alone.

The horses were ready in the square: King Anax and King Corylus would escort the black king to Palikè. Abeius went to meet Tuia with a gentle smile, something that until now the young elf had never noticed, but she was troubled in the soul: she had to talk to him and Gabrys, she needed to see her witch friend.

"Baby, you look upset … I think you need some rest."

"Abeius … where is Gabrys? I need to talk to you two together."

Abeius looked at her questioningly. He had sensed that there was some news, but he waited for her to talk about it, he didn't want to put pressure on her.

"Gabrys flew to the lakes of Naftia to pay homage to the Palics and to prepare the sacred judgment."

Then some laughter and cheerful chatter came from the path that led to the beach: they were Galateia and Salix who, happy, went up the road. Out of tune a bit feeling happiness in the air when Tuia felt so sad and Abeius sensed that she had so darkened because Salix had chosen another and not her.

"Let's go to the dragons, we'll fly with Typhoeus and Pendragon up to Palikè. We must arrive before the condemned because I have to talk to you "

She turned to the new couple and smiled thinly at them: "Long live love," she said, raising her hand to greet them before heading to the hill where the dragons sunbathed.

Pendragon and Typhoeus were ready, they took off immediately to the east and the red dragon also took off with them.

Tuia turned and saw it shining in the sun with its ruby scales and golden spine. It was really elegant.

"Typhoeus why is the red dragon following us? It could stay and rest in the sun."

"Uhm … She's a female dragon, her name is Zara."

"She's your girlfriend!" Tuia shouted excitedly.

"Girl … what? She chose me as her partner and I'm really happy about it."

Typhoeus seemed embarrassed.

"I too am very happy for you; you deserve so much happiness."

That news made the young elf happier or at least distracted her from her worries enough not to notice that they had already arrived at the Plain of Katanè.

They went down on Palikè, the air was cleaner and clearer than when she had been there for the first time: no sulphurous gases and steam banks, the ponds were quiet, all of the same identical shape strangely circular with a bubbling central of gurgling water.

Gabrys had already prepared seven fires around the ponds that she would use to burn magic herbs to render the water fumes harmless when the Palics would appear for the sentence: everything was ready and awaited the arrival of the elven caravan from Krastos with the condemned.

Tuia ran directly to her, she didn't even wait for Abeius who clumsily tried to get off Pendragon.

"Gabrys this morning by the sea I met Nereus and he told me about the sphere of thoughts of little Tuia."

"Why are you talking about the small Tuia sphere? It is your mind that was stolen … You are the same person: don't feel guilty for the child, you are the one who suffered this grave wrong and you are the only one who can save yourself."

"How do you know what the old man from the sea told me?" Tuia gasped, she didn't understand how Gabrys had guessed.

"I have been a druid for several centuries and then, you are the last-born elf, a Greener, guardian of fire, you are an important piece of this chessboard, aren't you? So, what else did he tell you?"

Gabrys managed to elicit a slight smile from Tuia's lips, giving her back that self-esteem that had failed her.

"So … he was from a certain oracle of the Cathedral Cave that told him to bring my sphere of thoughts, which the young Galateia had stolen from the monsters, directly to Selinos, to the temple of the Gorgons, where Medusa would have guarded it until the day I will go to take it back … Only I can do it."

Now it was Abeius and Gabrys who remained open-mouthed.

"And by the way, Echidna has become the supper of the Nereus' marine army and therefore, no pieces of monster to use for the Triskelion …"

In the last sentence Tuia accentuated all her disappointment, then turned and went to meet the elven cavalry that had just arrived at the Naftia ponds.

"What do you think about it?"Abeius turned to Gabrys suspiciously.

"I think it's not over yet. I am sure that something else has yet to happen," the bat replied resolutely, also going to Adranos's wagon.

All settled around the ponds, awaiting the arrival of the Palics. They had also placed huge baskets full of fruit and vegetables, eggs, and cheeses near the banks to thank the Palics for their presence.

Gabrys began to go around throwing leaves and dust on each of the braziers she prepared, when she reached the last one, the one next to the prisoner, she threw the leaves and turned to the center of the lake and said: "We await your judgment with respect and fear, magic brothers."

The two ponds began to boil fuming and spreading dense and dangerous vapors which however did not affect the guests because they were protected by the magic herbs of Gabrys. The banks of smoke and steam closed around those present: you could no longer see the plain of Katanè, nor could you see the great volcano.

Gabrys took from the hands of the condemned a tablet that had been given to him the night before to write his defense: it would have served the Palics to decide his fate.

From two huge geysers, two men dressed in white came out, one for each lake, so young that they looked like two little boys floating on the gurgling waters.

"Who did you bring?" the Palics, who just appeared from the ponds, whispered in unison.

"Adranos of Naxos, king of the Sicels."

Gabrys answered in a firm voice.

"Adranos of Naxos. The elves, as protectors of nature and peace of all living beings, have brought you in front of us. Imagine that to be here your brutality and your cruelty will certainly lead you to death."

Thus spoke the first brother.

"We will still allow you to explain yourself and to reveal to the judgment board your thoughts, your feelings, and what prompted you to generate similar atrocities, especially on defenseless beings."

Thus spoke the second brother.

Tuia watched Adranos, who had already lost all his power. He was trembling from head to toe and perhaps Abeius had been right in saying that he had always been a coward, allied with sea monsters only for fear of losing against the Phoenician people.

The elf then looked at her general of the hawks who had never wavered at anything, not even in front of the certainty of dying: he had passed under the judgment of the Palics and had come out unscathed, a symptom of fortitude, correctness and so much courage.

Lost in her thoughts she noticed only a few moments after the judgment tablet, from Adranos, floated towards one of the twins that he began to caress it. He did not read it, but he felt the writings with his palm and gathered the pleasant feelings or not that that piece of wood could suggest to him.

Then the tablet floated to the second brother who repeated the same movements that the twin had made, sniffed it and threw it in the water.

If the tablet had floated, Adranos would have been safe. A tense silence fell, everyone's eyes focused on that piece of wood that after five seconds went to the bottom like a stone.

Adranos began to scream like a madman, terrified and tried to escape, but from one of the lakes, a geyser rose up and sucked him into the depths of the water, bringing silence again.

Gabrys started her turn in the braziers again, showing the Palics the baskets full of gifts. Arriving near Tuia, she noticed that the young Greener had her eyes full of tears: the scene had been too strong for her. The witch said nothing to her and continued her tour to finish the celebration of the judgment.

The Palics stood still in their white robes, watching what the elves had given them, a faint smile on their face and the air of eternal kids.

They spoke to Tuia by thought before going.

“Don’t be upset dear sister. Remember: the judgment was legitimate. We’ll see you again.”

She looked up and met their, gleaming looks of emeralds of two Greeners of Air, of those she now considered brothers, smiled and they disappeared among the bubbling of those suphfurous waters.

Chapter XXIV

Tuia knew what she had to do, and where she had to go, yet in her heart, before leaving for Selinos, she had to see and talk to a person.

"Abeius, I want to go and say goodbye to Queen Thalia. She deserves to meet me one last time. I already know that if I go to Selinos I will never come back again."

Those words were a boulder on her stomach. She took a deep breath so as not to cry and lowered herself to tie her sandals, not even needing it: she could not look her general in the face, she had discovered that to think of leaving him was too painful.

"Certainly Tuia, I will accompany you if you want."

Abeius caressed her with his eyes, trying to remain calm so as not to upset her even more.

Gabrys approached them silently, she knew that the moment could be unsuitable, but she had to warn Abeius that she was leaving: "We have to organize the arrival in Selinos. I'm going to talk to King Anax and King Corylus, see you tomorrow morning in Krastos."

The words of the bat witch were like blades in the heart of Tuia who turned to prevent them from noticing her sad expression. Her gaze went to the valley, the plain of Katané that stretched green beneath her, and to the Ionius sea, of an intense blue that reminded her of the eyes of General Salix, that elf who had kidnapped her with her gentle manner and that by now it seemed only a child's flirtation.

Now Tuia felt changed, grown-up. Those days, she didn't know how many, she hadn't even managed to count them, those intense hours spent in a different world, risking her life for justice, for the peace of all without distinction of race or people, had shaped her mind. Now the fire of Etna burned inside her, incandescent lava flowed in her blood, her island lived inside her as she had never heard it before.

The elven caravans left. A little further north, King Corylus to reach the Green Valley of Alcantara, his hawks would have reached their families and finally breathed serenity after so many centuries.

King Anax was eager to return to his kingdom of Pantalica further south where he would reembrace his beloved wife and daughters; the elves of the hawthorn would find a kingdom in celebration honor of the return of their beloved queen and elven princesses.

Tuia and Abeius watched them go away, then climbed on their dragons again and flew towards the volcano.

Abeius and Pendragon waited a little farther from the crater, they were not allowed to penetrate the volcano, Tuia and Typhoeus instead entered without difficulty, after all, it was their "home."

The flames greeted the elf and the dragon jumping joyfully, shouting: "Long live the queen and the dragon Typhoeus, welcome back."

Tuia smiled at those little men of fire, they made her tenderness even though she knew they could be dangerous little beings, certainly not for her, but their appearance could be deceiving.

In all the confusion of shouts and cheerful ballets, Tuia did not notice Queen Thalia, who ran to her sobbing, suddenly embraced her, squeezing her tightly: "I didn't think of seeing you again, my daughter."

"M … Mother, Adranos is dead, I came back because I wanted you to know. The Palics, your children, my brothers have decided the legitimate punishment for him."

Tuia tried to remain detached in telling the facts to her adoptive mother but she would not have told her anything about Adranos's sad face when she had heard of his wife: Tuia had felt the sadness that had seized her when the death sentence arrived … Perhaps could that man still be saved? Or had the punishment chosen for him been right?

"Tomorrow is the big day and you will go away my daughter … But remember, as long as you carry the Trinacria inside you, you will always stay here with us."

Queen Thalia spoke softly to her, stroking her red hair like fire and her thin, pale face where small freckles stood out. Then she looked into her green eyes and whispered, gently searching for the right words:

"Adranos loved you so much Tuia, he dedicated the kingdom to you. I could not have children and for my love, he welcomed you as his sole heir. The Eastern Trinacria is yours by inheritance and you are the worthy sovereign. I am convinced that sometimes too much love turns into hatred, perhaps out of pride, jealousy or fear… What happened to that man we will never know, will remain forever preserved on the bottom of the Naftia ponds."

Tuia listened to the kind words of Queen Thalia, she did not judge the actions of the man who had betrayed her to obtain immortality from the notorious monsters, indeed she sought the reason for such behavior, but she felt her great sadness even though her words were dry, without tears.

While stroking her long hair Queen Thalia wove a thin red braid: "Cut this lock of hair for me, it will be a promise of return, because you will come back to me, my daughter."

Tuia took a small knife that she kept hidden in the sandal strap, cut the braid that Queen Thalia had created, and gave it to her. She took it, kissed it, and then tied it to her left wrist. "On the side of the heart," she said with a delicate smile.

"Mother I wanted to ask you to return to Naxos to be a guide for the Sicel people. Reign as the correct and loyal person you are, I can't do it, you already know it. You have suffered enough, Typhoeus and the dragons will always be ready to defend you and Etna will look at you from above and that look will be mine … I free you from the vow made to the volcano."

Queen Thalia nodded without speaking, and only gave her an elegant bow. "Now go, tomorrow will be an important day. I will wait for you forever."

She hugged her and kissed her on the cheeks without a tear in that farewell. Tuia appreciated it a lot, then the queen turned, slowly crossed the flames, and disappeared to the bottom of the cave, where once she had found a sleeping dragon.

Tuia was confused, there was something she did not understand or perhaps she was not aware of.

"Typhoeus, is there something I don't know? Everyone awaits tomorrow as if it was a day already predestined as if everyone already knew what was going to happen."

"In fact, it is exactly like this: tomorrow is an important day because it is designated by an ancient ogamic prophecy and your return to Trinacria has meant that this will come true."

"Prophecy? What prophecy? And why am I not aware of it?"

"Because the prophecy speaks of you and you will never be able to hear its words."

Typhoeus tried to be quite vague, he understood that Tuia was starting to get nervous because she wanted to know more.

"Let's go, Abeius and Pendragon wait." The golden dragon told her, changing the subject.

"Of course," replied Tuia. She still had her eyes turned to where she had seen Queen Thalia disappear, maybe she hoped to see her again, she was sorry she hadn't called her "mother", if only to give her joy, but that word hadn't come out of her heart, so maybe it was better not to utter it.

She said goodbye to the flames that had circled her and managed to climb up the Typhoeus saddle, then jumped off the cliff and took flight towards Krastos. Abeius and Pendragon followed them westward.

It was late afternoon when they arrived and found a party town: banquets and games had been set up in the rubble, and the children ran happily here and there playing with the "strummule", small spinning wooden tops that the old Sicans built with their hands, baskets of flowers adorned the square where a condemned man had been there early in the morning. On the beach, fires were lit, and the musicians and singers prepared their music and their traditional ballads.

Elymians and Sicans were happy, some were prepared for the party and others who had already begun to rebuild and clean up the rubble. From the east the Sicel people began to arrive, having heard the news of the death of Adranos, had come to honor the new queen and help the inhabitants of Krastos to revive the city.

When Tuia and Abeius went down the hill where Typhoeus and Pendragon had landed, they were amazed by the joyful reception of all those people: those who threw flowers, those who offered them drinks, the musicians began with their cheerful music, all danced and celebrated cheerfully.

The Sican's queen called Tuia and showed her an elegant tent that she had made fit for her, Tuia could rest and get ready for the big party in the evening by choosing from the wonderful clothes that the queen had brought for her.

Abeius went to the beach to sit on a small hill to admire the preparations and the sunset, but obviously, he was thinking of tomorrow.

"The day will touch the night and the night will touch the day." He whispered those words without realizing it.

"From the sacrifice of three, at midday, the Triskelion will be reborn and bring life to become the heart of the island, which will throb with fiery blood..." Typhoeus had come near him whispering the rest of the prophecy.

"Typhoeus stay with her until the end, I will not be allowed to enter the temple of the Gorgons," said the General of the Hawks without looking away from the sunset.

"Certainly, until the end," Typhoeus replied, honored by the words of Abeius.

Then the drums began to roll: the festivities were about to begin.

The king and queen of the people brothers, Elymians and Sicans, were in the center of the square with Tuia beside; in front of them the generals Mozio and Inico were receiving an investiture as governors, they would be assigned two cities to rebuild and administer.

"Elymians and Sicans, today is an important day because the elves and men have returned allies again after 300 years. This morning at dawn King Anax of the kingdom of Pantalica, king Corylus sovereign of the green Valley of Alcantara, and I Cocalo with my consort Lays, as sovereigns of the united peoples of the Elymians and Sicans, we signed an alliance pact. Now the queen of the Sicel people, the Greener Tuia, will seal the pact with her signature by combining the whole Trinacria, from Cape Pelorus, to Cape Lilybaeum to Cape Pachynum."

Tuia leaned down on the parchment resting on a small wooden table and signed the alliance pact.

She spoke emotionally: "This is a unique moment for our Island, this peace is the most precious thing you will have: know how to honor it, respect yourself and respect any race, be it animal, human or elven. That said, I would like to inform you that my mother, Queen Thalia of Naxos, will sit on my throne."

A chorus of amazement arose from the people who listened to Tuia's words, not expecting Queen Thalia to be alive after almost two hundred years.

"I imagined your surprise. On the evening of the Phoenician attack, the night of the betrayal of Adranos, Queen Thalia fled to the volcano, offering her soul to the dragon. That promise made her immortal.

This morning I freed my mother from that chain that bound her to Etna: she has already suffered enough; she must return to Naxos and lead the Sicel people. No one dares touch my kingdom or the fury of the dragons will break loose on the invaders."

Tuia finished speaking and general exultation hit her, the party had begun.

Abeius ran to her and gave her a clumsy bow and took her hand.

"Green looks good on you," he said kindly referring to the elegant dress that Queen Lays had given Tuia for the occasion, she wore a simple and elegant green silk dress and white flowers on her long red hair.

The hawks' general took her into the crowd and started dancing with her, something he had never done with anyone else in his life.

A large bat flew over them for a few seconds and then disappeared into the trees of the forest that surrounded the city of Krastos.

Salix in a high and elegant uniform danced with his sweet nereid Galateia, Tuia watched them dance a little: they were really beautiful together, then her eyes opened wide:

"Abeius … but are you dancing?"

Abeius smiled at her but didn't answer, he wanted to enjoy that last night with his beautiful elf.

They ate so many good things and for each fruit, Tuia tried to imprint its color, taste, and smell in her mind. She looked everyone in the face to remember them, but she had difficulty looking at her general, she tried in every way not to meet his eyes.

They joked and danced all evening until some fires on only a few red coals remained on the beach.

It was late at night and Tuia and Abeius were sitting in front of an almost off-bonfire looking at the stars.

"Abeius, I'll lose you again," Tuia whispered sadly.

"You will never lose me," the elf replied in a whisper, then he took the small necklace with the small pinecone from a small bag and tied it around her neck. "This is my promise."

Tuia felt happy and confident and fell asleep exhausted in the arms of her general.

Chapter XXV

"Little flame wake up, we have to go."

Tuia opened her eyes and saw Gabrys talking to her softly, she was in her bed in the tent that Queen Lays had built for her.

She jumped out of bed and went to look out of her tent, three delegations were ready: the elves of the hawthorn with King Anax, the queen Vitalba and the daughters Daisy and Robinia who greeted her smiling, the elves of the Green Valley of Alcantara with kings Corylus and Queen Silene, the Elymians and Sicans led by King Cocalo and his wife Queen Lays.

"They are all waiting for you to leave for Selinos; the dragons have already left to eliminate the Graias, the old monsters who guard the temple of the Gorgons, await our arrival there." Gabrys was anxious and agitated.

Tuia sat on her cot in silence, listening to the chatter outside her tent.

"I'd like to stay a little alone," she said to Gabrys.

The witch looked at her hesitantly, then decided to consent to her request to give her time to think.

Tuia wore the armor created for her by her mother, Queen Vitalba and the two princesses of the kingdom of hawthorn, took the sheath and took out the black metal sword received from King Corylus. Under her armor, she had her precious pinecone, a sign of Abeius' promise to always be there. Only then did she come out of the tent in her golden uniform that glistened in the sun, leaving everyone speechless with such beauty.

Abeius approached her.

"Will we go on horseback or on foot? He asked, smiling.

"We will run together."

Tuia answered with a smile on her lips, then turned to the east and raised her sword to greet Etna, who smoked profusely. She sheathed her weapon and set off swiftly south with her general next to her.

The three delegations moved on horseback, behind the two elves. Tuia breathed, she tasted the air as much as she could, she wanted the flavors of her island to remain on her: now that she really knew it, she would never want to leave it. She ran and every now and then a tear fell to wet that beloved land, that land of which Abeius was the guardian. She thought of him and the strange feeling she felt growing inside her but could never reveal to him: for him, she was just a child, his little elf.

Perhaps an hour passed before they arrived on a small hill from which they could see the enormous temple of Selinos and the coast immediately behind it.

They stopped to contemplate it. The abode of the Gorgons was enormous with very tall columns; of that temple, Tuia remembered its ruins on a school trip.

Abeius held her close, wanted to tell her so much, but decided to wait, she had to go away, and he couldn't upset her by revealing his feelings.

"Never be afraid. You are the daughter of fire and you command the dragons; your soul is the Etna … Remember my words when you will feel down or discouraged by life."

He held her close to his chest. He would not have wanted to let her go but destiny had to be fulfilled as the prophecy told.

"Tuia, Abeius, come. Dragons are waiting for you and Typhoeus would like to spend some time with you, darling."

Gabrys was climbing the road that led to the temple of the Gorgons, signaling the two elves to hurry.

Abeius took Tuia by the hand and slowly approached the ten dragons that awaited them from dawn.

"Little flame, you have given me life and mine will be consecrated to you forever. My heart will be your heart." Typhoeus spoke to her lovingly and Tuia put her hand to her chest, where she had her dragon print.

Pendragon brought his muzzle close to Tuia's chest, as he did the first time, he saw it and then looked into her eyes: "Take care of yourself, great queen, great warrior."

The other dragons bowed to Tuia by respectfully greeting her and positioned themselves in a circle but distant from the temple of the Gorgons, except Typhoeus who would have accompanied her inside.

Meanwhile, the three groups of men and elves had arrived. Gabrys had the first delegation, that of King Corylus, placed around the temple, a second circle was created by the men, Elymians and Sicans, and the third by the elves of the hawthorn.

The three sovereigns remained beside Gabrys in front of the columns of the entrance to the temple and awaited the right moment.

"Tuia! Tuia, you won't leave without saying goodbye to us!" Rosewood ran towards Tuia, pulling the delicate Magnolia behind him. They practically dived into her, squeezing her hard and covering the elf with petals and leaves. Magnolia smelled of cyclamen and Tuia was moved: she knew that the little petal elf wanted to say farewell to her.

Tuia's heart was beating wildly, Abeius could hear its sound, he squeezed her again in a long and silent hug and Tuia could breathe the scent that had always encouraged her. Then Abeius lowered himself to look directly into her eyes: "Don't be afraid, go and fulfill the destiny of the Trinacria."

He kissed her gently on the forehead and then let her go. Abeius went to take his place in the circle and while Tuia e Typhoeus began to enter the temple, Gabrys began the ceremony.

"Three hundred today are here,

three hundred like the years of the curse of infertility,

a hundred for every king…"

Tuia could barely hear the screams of the witch, as she slowly passed the first colonnades, she only felt the beating of her heart that echoed in her head.

"Tell me Typhoeus, tell me something … I'm shaking so much." The young elf sought comfort in the voice of the great Typhoeus who accompanied her to her destiny.

"Gabrys will now tell the prophecy and all three hundred people outside will repeat in chorus with her … Careful. Stop, I saw a movement down there. Close your eyes, you'll see through mine because no one can petrify a dragon."

Typhoeus tried to reassure Tuia creating a connection that allowed her to see through his eyes.

Everything was unbelievably quiet and silent: only the muffled passes of Tuia and Typhoeus could be heard. Through the dragon's eyes, the young Greener could see a soft green light created by candles lit and scattered in the great hall.

Suddenly, on the sides of an altar, two braziers caught fire.

"And so, the last-born elf has finally arrived at the temple of the Gorgons. Your precious human thoughts are guarded by the head of our beloved sister Medusa. Come forward, guardian of the fire, your dragon will watch over you, as he watches over the volcano, because you are the Etna. Little elf we thank you for having freed the Trinacria from the wickedness of those parents who did nothing to save us from our cruel destiny, which made us beasts immortal, feared, and hated by all when once was not so. Come closer and do not fear."

Two hooded figures spoke: they were Stheno and Euryale and together they showed the altar where the head of the third sister, Medusa, who was sleeping, was lying; dozens of snakes like hair held the green sphere of Tuia's thoughts suspended.

Gabrys outside the temple began to recite the prophecy:

"The first day of August,
the constellation of the dragon
the last-born elf will give you.
On the midsummer day you will lose it and then the same day it will return.
The last day of the Eighth will touch the night and the night will touch
the day.
From the sacrifice of three, at midday,
the Triskelion will be reborn
to bring back life,
becoming the heart of the island
that will pulsate with fiery blood.
The queen will one day return by choosing the island,
which her heart of fire will have given her."

When the prophecy was over, everything became dark. Those present raised their eyes to the sky: the night had touched the day and the day the night, it was twelve o'clock on the thirty-first of August and in the sky, there was a total eclipse.

"It is the moment! Shouted the bat, raising her arms to the sky and greeting the miraculous event that had made the noon dark.

Inside the temple, Tuia gathered all her courage and touched the green sphere of thoughts. In that instant, the snakes released the green sphere that began to float in mid-air. The Gorgons grabbed Medusa's head and began to scream, Tuia raised her hands to her ears to not hear that agony.

Suddenly she heard it again: "Come home, my darling …" was his human father's worried voice.

"Dad, help me!" Tuia yelled in a panic.

Medusa opened her eyes and her horrible mouth, sucking in her sisters, the sphere of thoughts and Tuia in a frightening vortex of lightning and electric discharges.

For a terrible moment, it was only chaos, then Typhoeus found himself in silence with his eyes closed. When he opened them again, he already knew he could no longer find his little flame, but the astonishment was that on the altar, where before there was the head of Medusa and the sphere of thoughts of Tuia, now there was the Triskelion.

Typhoeus admired it, and moved. It was more precious than the most precious gem that could exist on earth and shone with a green light, that of the beloved Tuia eyes, the rarest elf in the whole world.

He picked up the Triskelion gently, walking slowly inside that temple where the Gorgons had sacrificed themselves to rebuild the symbol of life.

When Typhoeus came out of the colonnade, the sun lit up again the day: all those present approached him and he opened his big paw showing them the much-desired Triskelion.

They all rejoiced and embraced, crying, moved. Gabrys turned to Abeius and saw him motionless, shocked. She came over and hugged him tightly.

"Our little warrior made it, she came back home," said the witch, beating the hawks' general on his shoulders.

"That's not her house … she'll come back to me one day."

Abeius moved away from the bat and reached Typhoeus to go and admire the Triskelion.

"Abeius, wait! Is there anything I don't know?"

Gabrys ran after Abeius who smiled under his mustache: he could not reveal to anyone what the Palics had seen in his future.

All entered the temple; Gabrys rekindled the braziers and all the candles that were inside. Typhoeus placed the Triskelion above the altar where he had found it and started to leave but the witch called him back:

"Typhoeus wait, we are here to allow another prophecy to come true, which you obviously don't know … that it concerns you…

The Triskelion will be reborn to bring life back,

becoming the heart of the island,

which will beat with fiery blood."

Typhoeus stopped, his eyes widened and turned to look at Gabrys who had taken the Triskelion and showed it to him:

"Do you want to keep the Triskelion in your heart, oh great and majestic Etna's dragon?"

Typhoeus did not speak but opened the scales of his chest to show a pulsating fiery heart. Gabrys approached and gently placed the Triskelion inside, letting the dragon close over his golden scales.

Two huge tears came out of Typhoeus's big eyes, carrying Trinacria inside him along with Tuia's love for the island.

Someone under him was busy with some cruets, it was Rosewood who had decided that not even a dragon's tear had to be wasted, they were too precious.

While everyone congratulated the enormous golden dragon, a man ran screaming inside the temple:

"Run quickly! I need help…"

The blood of all those present froze. What could have happened again? They quickly followed that man who came down to the beach; on the shore, a small boat stopped. Abeius and Salix ran to check and noticed inside a woman, no, not a woman, but an elf and … she was giving birth.

"Hurry up women! Hurry up elf! A baby is about to be born here!" shouted Abeius cheerfully.

Gabrys and some women helped the young elf give birth while among the waves Nereus and his daughters followed the scene, happy to have accompanied the boat on that shore.

"The curse has been canceled! It's a girl! May the stars of heaven bless the firstborn elf! Her name will be SICILY …" shouted Gabrys, raising the baby in the air so that everyone could see her.

Now everyone smiled and passed that little pink bundle that had brought the future to the island. "Yes, I would say that Sicily will be the future of the island." Abeius smiled.

"Bat… I still have a few pieces of the monster gathered at Cape Pelorus. Do I leave them to you? Maybe you can make a soup out" The elf general grinned at a stunned Gabrys.

Then he asked her seriously.

"Now what will you do?"

Gabrys sat on a hill of sand, scanning the horizon. "I'd say I'll sit here and smoke my pipe in peace waiting for my Orry."

Abeius turned and began to climb the sand dunes; from afar Typhoeus and Pendragon were waiting for him.

Chapter XXVI

"Tuia …"

"Dad…" Tuia answered almost in a hiss before opening her eyes.

"You are back, my daughter! You were brave, I'm proud of you."

Mr Carlo whispered in her ear.

Tuia opened her eyes and was blinded by the neon light, then read on the wall right in front of her "UMBERTO I HOSPITAL COMPANY, SYRACUSE" and under the date "September 23, 2018".

She smiled.

"Happy Birthday Daddy."

Glossary

Triskelion or triskellion or Trinacria is the symbol of Sicily. The symbol of the Trinacria is now known because it is present in the flag of Sicily and that of the Isle of Man. Its history is articulated and, in some ways, still shrouded in mystery, or in any case in vagueness, because it is linked to mythology. The trinacria, symbol of Sicily, is composed of the head of the Gorgon, whose hair is snakes intertwined with ears of wheat, from which radiate three legs bent at the height of the knee. The Gorgon is a mythological figure, which according to the Greek poet Hesiod (VIII - early VII century BC) was each of the three daughters of Forcys and Ceto, two sea gods: Medusa (the Gorgon par excellence), Stheno ("the strong"), Euryale ("the spacious"). Sicily is still called Trinacria today.

Abeius, general elf of the falcons of King Corylus of the Green kingdom of Alcantara. Greener, guardian of the earth.

Abola, ancient name of Avola, a town in south-eastern Sicily, known for the production of wine "Nero d'Avola."

Adranos, king of the Sicel people, governs the whole of Eastern Sicily, from north to south, up to the river Hymera (Salso).

Akragos, was an ancient city on the southern coast of the island of Sicily, today's Agrigento.

Alice, Tuia's little sister, two years younger.

Anaktoron, is the name of the castle of the king of elves Anax of the kingdom of Pantalica, located on Mount Lauro.

Anapo, L'Anapo is a river of Sicily that flows in south-eastern Sicily. The name, in ancient Greek, means invisible and derives from the fact that in many points of its path the Anapo gets swallowed up in the subsoil, disappearing from sight.

Anax, the elf king of the kingdom of Pantalica, is symbolized by the hawthorn.

Bats' cave, located at the northern end of Pantalica. It looks like a wide arch carved into the rock and is the largest natural cave in the area. Its name is due to the presence of bats that live inside the bowels of this cave, characterized by beautiful columns, stalactites and stalagmites. Locally it is called as "*A Rutta 'e Taddariti.*"

Branchiere dog, molossoid dogs, Sicel-bred.

Carlo Castello, father of Tuia.

Cathedral Cave, at about thirty meters, in the depths of the Mediterranean Sea opens this cave which gives the sensation of being in a Gothic cathedral. In remote times emerged from water as evidenced by the numerous stalactites and stalagmites that can be admired inside. It is located in Marettimo, the Egadi island belonging to Sicily, in the Mediterranean Sea.

Charybdis, sea monster, which infested the waters of the Strait of Messina.

Cape Lilybaeum, extreme north-west tip of Sicily.

Cape Pachynum, extreme south-eastern tip of Sicily.

Cape Pelorus, extreme north-eastern tip of Sicily.

Faria Cave, located on the opposite wall of the highest "Cave of bats", is a cave of the kingdom of Pantalica.

Ceto, sea monster, sister of Nereus. She married her brother Phorcys and gave him many sons: Echidna, Scylla, Graeae, Ladon and Gorgons. Ceto was the embodiment of the dangers of the sea and the hidden fears.

Cocalo, King of the United People of the Elymians and Sicans.

Corylus, king of the elves of the Green Valley of Alcantara, its symbol is the peregrine falcon.

Daisy, elf daughter of King Anax and Queen Vitalba.

Devil, name of one of the dogs, Branchiere dogs of King Adranos.

Doride, Nereus' wife with whom she had 50 daughters.

Draconic, is the language of dragons written and spoken mainly by dragons.

Echidna, sea monster daughter of Ceto e Phorcys.

Elen síla lúmenn' omentielvo (elfic), a star shines at the time of our meeting.

Elymians, an ancient population that lived in the western part of Sicily.

Ellan Vannin, ancient name of the Isle of Man.

Emma, Tuia's mom.

Erin, the ancient name of Ireland.

Etna, Etna is the highest active volcano in Europe and is located in north-eastern Sicily.

Etnah, name of the sword of Tuia created by the meteor from which she was born.

Euryale, one of the Gorgons daughters of the Ceto and Phorcys sea monsters.

Flames, flame elves that lived inside the volcano Etna.

Gabrys, the druid or witch of the kingdom of Pantalica, friend of King Anax and called "the bat."

Galateia, Nereid, one of Nereus' 50 daughters.

Graeae, also known as Forcidi, were the daughters of Phorcys and Ceto and sisters of the Gorgons. They were called Enio and Penfredo. They represented the various moments of old age: in fact, they had never been young and had only one eye and one tooth in common. They guarded the access to the temple where their sisters, the Gorgons, lived.

Green Valley of Alcantara, natural canyon, unlike what is commonly thought, has not been dug over thousands of years by water. The Alcantara river flows through the lava stone that forms its characteristic bed.

Gorgons, they are monsters and they were daughters of Phorcys and Ceto. They were three sisters, Stheno, Euryale and Medusa.

According to the myth, the Gorgons had the power to petrify anyone with their gaze and Medusa was the only one not to be immortal. Medusa and her sisters were depicted as horrendous women with gold wings and bronze hands, with a round face framed by a mass of hair snakes.

Gurth goth rim lye (elfic), to death our enemies.

Halykos, the ancient name of the Platani river, is one of the most important waterways on the southern side of Sicily.

Hymera, ancient name of the Salso River that flows in central Sicily.

I amar prestart aen, han mathon ne nen, han maton ne chae a han noston ne 'wilith (elfic), the world has changed, I can feel it in the water, I can feel it in the earth, I can breathe it in the air.

Inessa, female peregrine falcon friend of Abeius.

Inico, General of the Sicans.

Ionian Sea, north of Sicily.

Katan, peregrine falcon friend of Abeius.

Katanè, ancient name of the city of Catania that rises at the foot of the volcano Etna.

Krastos, was a city of ancient Sicily on the Sican Mountains.

Ladon, sea monster son of Ceto e Phorcys.

Lays, Queen wife of King Cocalus of the United People of the Elymians and Sicans.

Madonie, are a short mountain range located in the northern part of Sicily.

Magnolia, petal elf of the kingdom of Pantalica, changes flower scent according to the feelings she has.

Malus, name of one of the dogs, Branchiere dog of King Adranos.

Mediterranean Sea, south of Sicily.

Medusa, one of the Gorgons daughters of the sea monsters Ceto and Phorcys.

Mountain Lauro, is a mountain of south-eastern Sicily belonging to the Iblei Mountains, of which it is the highest peak. On Mount Lauro was built the castle of King Anax, the majestic Anaktoron.

Mountain Tauro, is located in an elevated position with respect to Naxos, under Etna, where stands the black castle of Adranos.

Mountains Erei, are located in the center of Sicily.

Mountains Hiblaean, are located in the south-eastern part of Sicily.

Mountains Nebrodi, a mountain range in northern Sicily.

Mountains Peloritans, are a mountain range of north-eastern Sicily.

Mountains Sicans, are a mountain range that is located in the central-southern area of Sicily.

Mors, name of one of the dogs, Branchiere dog of King Adranos.

Motyon, was a small town or fortress of ancient Sicily, was born between the river Hymera (Salso) and Platani (Halykos).

Mozio, general of the people of the Elymians.

Mulciber, peregrine falcon friend of Abeius.

Naftia lakes, are located in the plain of Catania (Katanè). Until the emission activity was bridled, the lake was "double", composed of two side by side crater basins. From the surface bubbles of carbon dioxide, hydrogen and methane constantly gush out as two or three jets of water rise and are dragged upwards by the pressure of the gases. The colour of the water is yellow-greenish.

Naxos, capital city of the Sicel kingdom where the castle of King Adranos stood.

Nereus, wise man who lives in the depths of the sea, brother of the monsters Ceto and Phorcys, with prophetic gifts has fifty daughters called Nereids. Greener, guardian of the water.

Netum, Noto Antica or Netum, is the ancient village of Noto destroyed by the earthquake of January 11, 1693.

Ogamic, is a type of writing that was used to transcribe ancient Celtic languages.

Old Mountain, Old Mountain is a vast isolated relief with sheer walls, located on the Sicans mountains.

Orry, king of the Isle of Man elves.

Orto, name of one of the dogs, Branchiere dog of King Adranos.

Palics, twin sons of Queen Thalia, born from a spell, their birth caused the boiling of the waters of Lake Naftia, of which they became the highest judges. Greeners, air guardians.

Palikè, The archaeological site of Palikè, famous in antiquity as the seat of the sanctuary of the Palics brothers.

Pantalica, or rather the Rock Necropolis of Pantalica, is a naturalistic-archaeological site. The site is located on a plateau south-east of Sicily, surrounded by canyons formed over the millennia by two rivers, the Anapo and the Calcinara, which have determined the orography of the canyon.

Perseids, constellation protector of elves and men.

Pendragon, majestic black dragon, boss of all dragons of Ireland (Erin).

Peninsula of Thapsos, the archaeological area of Thapsos is one of the most important sites of the Middle Bronze Age in Sicily located in the Magnisi Peninsula in south-eastern Sicily.

Phorcys, marine monster husband of Ceto, represents the dangers hidden in the depths of the sea.

Robinia, elf daughter of King Anax and Queen Vitalba, their firstborn.

Rosewood, leaf elf of the kingdom of Pantalica.

Salix, general elf of the hawthorn in the kingdom of Pantalica of King Anax.

Scylla is a sea monster, daughter of the Phorcys and Ceto monsters.

Segesta, a city in western Sicily.

Selinos was an ancient Greek city on the south-western coast of Sicily; today it is the largest archaeological park in Europe, called Selinunte.

Seed of genesis, a small cone found in the left hand of Tuia, when the constellation of the dragon sent her to earth.

Sicily, Sicily, the largest island in the Mediterranean, is located in the extreme south of Italy.

Sicels, ancient population of eastern Sicily.

Silene, elven queen of the Green Valley of Alcantara, wife of King Corylus.

Silva, blind druid of the Green Valley of Alcantara, sword-maker.

Stheno, one of the Gorgons, daughter of Ceto e Phorcys.

Symaithos, the ancient name of the river Simeto that rises on the Nebrodi mountains in the north-east of Sicily and flows around the volcano Etna and then flows into the Mediterranean Sea.

Thalia, Queen of Sicels, King Adranos' wife.

The Sicans, ancient population of central Sicily.

Tyrrenous Sea, north of Sicily.

Typhoeus, a dragon with golden scales that lives inside the volcano Etna. Greener, guardian of the fire, was the dragon that by mistake destroyed the Triskelion.

Vicio, Sicans pastor asking for help from the elves.

Vitalba, elven queen of the kingdom of Pantalica.

War, name of one of the dogs, Branchiere dog of King Adranos.

Zara, female ruby red dragon, from Ireland (Erin).

The song of Abeius is taken from the song "Guerriero" by Marco Mengoni

Biographical Note

Roberta Randone, aka Roby R., was born in April 1977 in Syracuse in Sicily, the largest island in the Mediterranean Sea. Attracted by mythology and fantasy, since she was a child, she has written fantastic stories and tales to give as gifts to relatives and friends. Lover of nature, for several years she was President of a non-profit environmental association that militates in the Sicel territory against the abuses of large industries.

She emigrated to London in 2015 and began to attend New City College, where, studying English, she rediscovered her desire to return to writing thanks to the encouragement of her tutor and English teacher Rama Diagne, whom she described as "The lighthouse that illuminated her path." Thanks to Rama, Roby R. participates in the "Word Book Night Writing Competition" where she wins first place with a short story in English, awarded by writer and director Michael Marshall Smith. Thus, began her career as a writer, with a fantasy saga entitled "The world in elfic eyes", where mythology, history and fantasy frame childhood stories lived in her beloved island, Sicily.

All the places told are real, to help the reader identify with places and situations experienced by the characters. Roby R. is the name that has followed her childhood and that has marked her life as president, that part of herself warrior and imaginative that has always helped her to fight reality, often difficult and sometimes even cruel.

"I've always loved to write, and I think it takes courage to write a book. I always wanted to do it, but I was weak psychologically, unable to think I could do it. Triskelion for me was like a flight on a glider from Everest, exciting and scary. I emigrated to London from Sicily, taking with me a strong resentment towards my land, then meeting other immigrants, from the most remote areas of the world who spoke with love of their origins, praising everything about their land, I began to reflect on what I had inside me.

When they asked me to talk about my native land, I could not help but talk about the sea, the flavours and smells of my island, Sicily. And so, I understood that the fire of my land was still inside me, I lived and carry in blood and bone my island and I would like anyone to rediscover it differently as I rediscovered it, starting from its origins.

"Sicily, in this way, has never been told."

The Italian version of
"The World In The Eyes Of An Elf-Triskelion"
has received these awards:

II place, International prize "Navarro",
Sambuca di Sicilia

Culture Award at the "Golden Dickens Awards 2020"
in Naples

SPECIAL JURY AWARD,
INTERNATIONAL POETRY AND NARRATIVE
AWARD
"CITTA 'DI LATINA AWARD"

Available worldwide online
and from all good bookstores

Michael Terence
Publishing

www.mtp.agency

www.facebook.com/mtp.agency

@mtp_agency

CPSIA information can be obtained
at www.ICGtesting.com
Printed in the USA
LVHW041653261122
734044LV00004B/107

9 781800 944510